PRAISE FOR TONY DUNBAR
AND
THE TUBBY DUBONNET MYSTERY SERIES

"A STUPENDOUS SERIES."
—*Midwest Book Review*

"A REMARKABLE FEEL FOR LOCAL COLOR is the great strength of Tony Dunbar . . . and Dubonnet [is] a lovable, wisecracking eccentric who has an uncanny ability to track down other eccentrics living on the wrong side of the law."
—*Baltimore Sun*

"Tony Dunbar brings his own vision of the Big Easy in his Tubby Dubonnet novels . . . [which] combine the caper with the hard-boiled mystery, and a good dash of humor."
—*Ft. Lauderdale Sun-Sentinel*

"The wacky but gentle sensibilities of Tubby Dubonnet reflect the crazed, kind heart of New Orleans better than any other mystery series."
—*New Orleans Times-Picayune*

"DUNBAR CATCHES
OF NEW ORLEANS
—*Pub*

Lucky
Man

TONY DUNBAR

A Dell Book

Published by
Dell Publishing
a division of
Random House, Inc.
1540 Broadway
New York, New York 10036

ISBN: 0-440-22662-7

Printed in the United States of America

Published simultaneously in Canada

December 1999

10 9 8 7 6 5 4 3 2 1

OPM

To Mary Price,
whose understanding and love
make all things possible.

Acknowledgments

Thanks to Marilu O'Byrne, Joshua Nidenberg, and Jesse Beach, who have filled glaring gaps in my knowledge, to Pat Brady, and Steve Sullivan for their slants on New Orleans, to Hugh Knox and Linda Kravitz for their encouragement throughout, and especially to my editor, Jackie Cantor.

1

"I don't know why you have to be difficult," Raisin Partlow told his date. "You said you wanted to go out on the town."

"This is not 'town.' This is crackville!" Her arms were crossed and she wouldn't get out of the car.

"This is the Irish Channel, honey. Forget about crackville. You're safe as can be," he coaxed.

She wasn't having it. "There's a sign right there on that house that says SLUM PROPERTY. Does that tell you anything?"

"That's some stupid thing the city bureaucrats put up. I've been coming to this bar all my life. Trust me. You'll like it."

The din inside was deafening. Men and women shouted and shoved, waving fistfuls of money in the air to get their bets down. Raisin pushed forward through the smoky haze until he reached the center of the action, dragging his reluctant companion behind him. A space had been cleared on the floor, brightly illuminated by a fluorescent light. You could barely hear the chicken clucking.

"Black ten, black ten," he cried, trying to keep a grip on his girlfriend.

One hundred numbered squares were painted on the tavern's cement floor. Resting over them was a big wire cage, like a giant crab trap, inside of which a flustered chicken hopped about and scratched.

"This way, little darlin'!"

"Don't be shy!"

"Now, now, now!"

They pleaded with the bird and whooped and hollered. Somebody slammed into Raisin's back and gave him a drunken hug when he protested. A barmaid dispensing potions from her tray poked him in the side, elbowing her way through the excited throng. His date got lost for a moment. Raisin looked down and found her on the floor, trying to grab his leg, sputtering at him.

Laughing, Raisin pulled her up and tried to ignore her fist pounding on his chest.

Finally the fowl's gullet quivered. Her feathers shook politely, and she carefully shat.

"Red number eighty-two!" the master of the game proclaimed, unleashing a chorus of groans and threats upon the bird's life, but the proof was unmistakably there.

The proprietor's burly arm reached in and retrieved the bird, which he cradled protectively against his chest.

"Settle up at the bar," he called out to quiet the crowd. "Next drop in one hour."

At his signal a nephew tugged a rope and lifted the cage up to the ceiling. The chicken was carried to the back room, where her reward of fresh pellets and bread pudding awaited.

Patrons walked over the game board to verify the result until the evidence was ground away by countless feet.

"That's certainly a rare form of entertainment," Raisin exulted. "You won't see that every day."

"You are too crude for words," his date said. "Take me home, and I mean it."

Outside, a dog barked on the quiet street and chemical tank cars on the New Orleans Public Belt Railroad clanked together and slowly started to roll.

Raisin crushed his cigarette on the broken pavement and held the car door open for the woman.

"I guess that was your first chicken drop," he said, trying to get a conversation going.

She slammed the door.

She's a moody one, Raisin thought.

"It's always like this when we work together," Johnny Vodka complained. "Your car breaks down and we're on the bus."

"Not every time. Last time we rode in a cab."

"We drove a cab. That was our cover. And you ran over a lady's Chihuahua."

"So? The department paid for it."

"You're always focusing on money. I'm talking loss of life."

"A Chihuahua is life?"

They were still debating this issue when the bus let them off at the end of the line. Aging brick apartment buildings arranged like orange boxes squatted on hard-packed earth, beaten flat by generations of little children and police car tires.

Johnny Vodka and his partner Frank Daneel walked across the first yard they came to, pool sticks in one hand and duffel bags in the other. A couple of sharks coming for a private weekend in the super's secret vice den—that was the charade. They dumped it all in a heap in front of a featureless concrete facade while Daneel went to a door marked 3-G and knocked.

Johnny "V" stepped around the corner to light a cigarette out of the wind and to gaze upon the barren landscape, dotted with pockets of people, a group of children playing with a soccer ball, fat ladies clustered in a circle on folding chairs.

They were supposedly working undercover, but he could tell that they stuck out like sore thumbs.

He looked over his shoulder and watched a scrawny female going through his luggage. It took him a moment to realize that she was brazenly stealing from him.

"Hey!" he yelled, and tried to grab her.

Quick as a lizard she snagged a pool cue and darted away toward a playground where guys hustled chess and old men played bourre.

Instinctively Johnny picked up the remaining stick and charged after her. His long strides gave him a chance, and he cornered her behind an overgrown bush.

The panting woman feinted one way and then the other, trying to get him off balance so she could run past him. She was twenty, maybe, pretty, and had wild black hair and a dress flecked with sweat.

Then they both jumped the same way. The policeman almost got a hand on her and then almost lost it when she swung her stick wickedly at his wrist.

Johnny raised his own cue in self-defense, and hers cracked down with a loud pop. To his amazement she threw away her broken stick and had the gall to spit at him. Then she shot him a bird and tried to sprint away again.

Angry and flushed, Johnny whipped the pole across her butt and knocked her flat on the ground. When he reached for her ankle she scrambled away like a crab and, holding her thigh in pain, hissed at him.

"Get lost." Vodka cursed, giving it up.

While he dusted off his pants she danced away down the sidewalk, gleeful in escape, until she almost collided with the glassy-eyed tall man. He beckoned her forward and grinned.

The girl froze, while Johnny watched her out of curiosity. She backed up. The tall man took a step toward her, and that was all.

Like a dove flushed from cover the woman raced back toward the policeman, arms waving madly in the air.

She jumped on him and gave him a hug so tight, he

could feel her breasts through his shirt and smell the French fries in her hair.

"Help me, please," she begged.

Johnny Vodka looked over her head, but the tall man was gone. He wished he had paid more attention to what the guy looked like.

2

It was a blazing hot autumn day, and the natives stayed indoors. So vivid was the lush greenery, the purple of the crape myrtle, the turquoise and orange pastels of the tilted cypress houses, the cloudless blue sky—that even through a protective shield of glass, Tubby Dubonnet was almost blinded. He was having a cup of strong coffee with his daughter at a shop on St. Charles Avenue. Squinting, he stared past her bare shoulder at the cars passing on the street, thinking how bright this city was, how hot it was, while she conversed about her life.

"I don't know. He's just not the kind of guy you'd want to marry, if you know what I mean. He's real smart, though, straight B's, stuff like that, and lots of fun. He used to date Estelle. . . ." Christine paused to bite into an enormous cinnamon bun. At eighteen, barely, she had most of life figured out. "I think he just needs to mature," she continued, "and maybe he ought to move away from here for a while and see what the rest of the world is like. . . ."

Her father appreciated the intimacy, but he had lost track of who this story was about. Since he had quit drinking he had focused most of his erratic mental energy on work. Other things seemed a distraction because they reminded him of booze. And it was so blessed hot, his concentration was shot. Whatever beauty existed in this sleepy metropolis by the river surely vaporized at this temperature. It was almost Thanksgiving, for God's sake. Give us a break.

He watched a cabdriver stopped in traffic toss a crumpled-up Popeyes bag and an empty plastic soda bottle out of the window, just like that. A passing streetcar blew the bag across the pavement and into the gutter. The plastic bottle bounced along the street until another car flattened it. As the lawyer glared at his colorful, lazy city, all he could see was the trash.

"So, what do you think, Dad?" Christine checked her fingernails, knocked back some decaf iced coffee, and looked over the rim of her glass at him expectantly.

"I'm sorry, sweetheart. You want to know whether to date this guy?"

She looked at him in dismay.

"You know, I think maybe I'm getting too old for this place," he said, cutting off her protest.

She frowned. "You don't like the music they play, the coffee, what?"

"No, I mean New Orleans, the whole town."

"Lots of other old people live here, Daddy," she

said, meaning him, he supposed, though—in truth—Tubby was only forty-something.

He watched a bum, an old one, shuffle along the neutral ground looking for aluminum cans.

"Besides, the whole family lives in New Orleans. Where else could you go?"

He shrugged. His family was an ex-wife and three daughters getting on with their lives. "No place, I guess. Just a thought. Could be I'm just tired of working." Actually, he was just tired of not drinking. "Skip it. Tell me what's going on with you."

"Well, like I was saying"—she glanced at him with some exasperation—"it's a choice between staying out of school next year and trying to start a literary magazine or maybe transferring to the University of Albuquerque with . . ." He was gone again.

Across the street a police car double-parked so that the officer could drop his laundry off at the Nouveau Cleaners. Traffic snarled down the block. At the corner they were putting up a banner for something called Rite Aid to cover up what had once been a handsome purple advertisement for K & B Drugs. The old drugstore's beloved brilliant grape was being forever erased, except at Mardi Gras, from the New Orleans landscape. All of these events seemed to portend a greater collapse.

In his mind he was crossing a bridge and leaving New Orleans behind.

3

In a moment of weakness Tubby Dubonnet, basically a cautious person by virtue of his profession as a lawyer, had let Raisin Partlow move in. They were old pals, and Raisin's girlfriend had just kicked him out. It was supposed to be for a few days only, but time was grinding on.

Tubby drove his fat Chrysler LeBaron very fast as a general rule, but this afternoon, lost in thought, he was making a baby-blue streak down Claiborne Avenue. He felt cramped. His six-foot frame and broad shoulders felt compressed in the car. His law practice seemed too small and inadequate to nourish his brain in the days ahead. The recent assassination of the crime czar had removed one of life's purposes while at the same time leaving him curiously dissatisfied. His home was too populated, and not populated enough. Life was a drag.

A pothole jarred his teeth and brought him back to the present. Raisin was like a brother, but what were virtues in a friend were aggravating as hell around the house. Right now, he imagined that his lodger was probably lounging on the sofa watching the PGA tour, thinking no deep thoughts, and most likely swigging the bourbon Tubby had put out of sight when he forsook the bottle. Well, not quite forsook. He assured himself that he was just giving it up on a trial basis.

The lawyer had not had an enjoyable day. He had argued with two of his clients and had squandered four and a half nonbillable hours in court—where a judge had called him excitable. He was tired and stressed and had more kinks than Barq's root beer could smooth away. Whiskey was good. He remembered that much.

The vexed motorist made the turn onto Nashville Avenue, into the shelter of the live oak trees that covered the narrow street and usually restored calm. A noisy marching band in full crimson regalia paraded in the yard of the high school on the corner. Rows of brass instruments rose and fell in waves, and Big Chief thundered discordantly throughout the neighborhood, bringing wistful memories to shut-ins, but all Tubby noticed was that the long row of parked yellow school buses forced him to slow down.

The Roman Candy Man in his horse-drawn carriage, offering toffee chewing sticks at fifty cents a pop, was resting at the corner of Willow Street. This was a colorful sight that usually rated at least an appreciative pause, but today Tubby sailed past without a thought, so fast that the old nag shuddered in the draft.

A few brisk turns and he bumped into his own driveway. Briefcase under the arm, he nicked a finger trying to get the front door unlocked, capping a day of annoyances. He stepped into his living room and, just as he thought—suspicions confirmed.

"How's it going?" Raisin asked, eyes glued to the TV. He was relaxing on the couch, wearing sweats as though he might have spent the afternoon building up his physique. By his elbow was a green bottle of beer, making wet rings on one of Tubby's fishing magazines. The only missed prediction was that Raisin wasn't watching the sports channel—he was watching that damn video again.

"Fine, you?" Tubby asked gruffly. He tossed his worn briefcase on a chair.

"Oh, so-so." Raisin didn't look up. "Sure is hot outside," he said.

It was the tape that had fallen into Tubby Dubonnet's hands during the Sheriff Mulé case. The late sheriff's personal attorney had kept the item in his office safe. Its origin was unknown, but Tubby surmised its value lay in its potential for blackmailing someone. But who?

On the screen the young red-haired girl with freckles on her cheeks talked to the man with the soft voice whose face was never revealed to the camera. She was explaining her story for the hundredth time.

The lawyer shook his head and stomped off to the kitchen for a cold ginger ale. Furiously popping the top, he trudged upstairs to change.

Raisin had to go, he decided. The question was how to break it to him.

* * *

"I didn't think it would be strange," the woman with the red hair said, facing the camera as if it could help her. She rubbed her nose and looked down at her hands. She was seated at a small table. There were no decorations on the wall behind her.

"I never answered a personals ad before, but, you know, sometimes I'd read them. I really didn't know what to expect."

"But you answered this one." The man's voice had almost no inflection. Except for a faint ghost that sometimes moved on the wall behind the woman, her interrogator was invisible.

"Yes, I answered it. It seemed pretty interesting—all right, you know?"

"The ad appeared in *Gambit* on May the eighteenth?"

"I don't know. I think so."

"This is the copy of the ad you showed me?" A man's arm, curly black hairs running under a golden wristwatch and up to where the sleeve was rolled to the elbow, pushed a piece of paper across the table. A shadow fell over the woman and then disappeared.

"Sure, that's it."

"What does it say?"

"It says: Single white male, thirty-two, six feet tall, good job, good looking like Mel Gibson, lonely, seeking adventurous attractive single or divorced woman twenty-one to thirty-five, redhead preferred, for dining, dancing, sweet nothings, possible long-term relationship. It won't hurt to call.''

''That appealed to you?''

''Yeah, especially the part about red hair and dancing.''

''What did you do?''

''I answered the ad.''

''With a phone call.''

''Yeah. I called the number and, you know, left a message.''

''And?''

''I didn't think much about it, but he called me back a couple of days later.''

''At your house?''

''My apartment, actually.'' She brushed some hair off her forehead.

''What did he say?''

''Oh, he sounded great. He had a real nice voice. He came on as so sincere. He said maybe we should exchange photos. I said I didn't have one, which I didn't have a good one at the time. Then we talked some more. I remember he said he liked to swim and had a pool.''

''Then you made a date.''

''Yeah. Just for coffee, at a place on St. Charles Avenue. I think they call it Java, or something. He was late, so I just waited for him. They have TVs you can watch.''

''But he showed up?''

''Sure did.''

''Describe him, please.''

''Oh, he was good looking all right. Wavy black

hair. Not actually like Mel Gibson at all, but younger. He combs his hair back, like, with a mousse. He has a good tan. There's a dimple in his chin. Well built. What do you want me to say?''

"That's fine. What did he say his name was?''

"Harrell. Harrell Hardy. I don't think that's really his name.''

"What happened then?''

"We had coffee. We talked. He invited me out for dinner.''

"When?''

"That same night. We went straight from the coffee place. First we went out for drinks. I think it was called the Bombay Club. I've got the matches somewhere. Then some Italian place. I don't remember its name.''

"And?''

"And we're eating spaghetti, and he asks me do I dance. I say yes. He says did I ever do it professionally. I told him no, even though I do, sort of. I just didn't want to get into it, but . . . Anyhow, he says maybe I can learn, which I thought was odd. Then he asks what I think about escorting important men to parties.''

"Escorting?''

"That's his word. He said it paid extremely well, and it didn't have to involve, you know, sleeping with anybody. That was up to me.''

"What did you tell him.''

"That he was out of his fucking noodle.''

"And his response?''

" 'Just something to think about, doll. It's easy money.' ''

"After that you went to a hotel and had sex with him?"

"Do I have to say?"

"Sure. It's part of your complaint."

"Well, we didn't have sex right away, but, yeah. We did."

"After he'd asked you about the escort service."

"That's right. I didn't say I was proud of myself." She looked away from the camera, and when she turned back there was a tight smile on her lips as if she had just told herself a little joke.

"What happened then?" the voice asked.

"Another man came into the room and got into bed with us."

"And then?"

"I tried to get out of the bed. Nothing like that ever happened to me before, but they wouldn't let me."

"They raped you?"

"I'd say so."

"Well, did you resist, or did you consent?"

"I told them no way, but they were touching me all over my body, if you must know, and it's kind of hard to think straight in a situation like that."

"Okay, what happened?"

"Nothing. They did lots of things to me. I did lots of things to them. I'm not going to describe it in graphic detail. Later on the other man left. Then Harrell took me home. He gave me two hundred dollars and said it had been a great time."

"You took the money?"

"I tried not to."

"Well?"

"He stuck it between my . . . in my bra, and he rode off in his car before I could do anything about it."

"Did he call you again?"

"Yeah, a bunch of times. I didn't want to see him anymore."

"Why not?"

"Because I felt bad about what happened. It was very degrading, and I didn't want it to happen again."

"Why did you report it to us?"

"Because I don't want somebody else to get tricked like that. You read these personals, you think that something good might happen for you. You get to dreaming. It's not fair."

"How old are you?"

"I turned eighteen last week."

"You were seventeen when this occurred?"

"Right. What's the difference?"

"If you were a little younger, it wouldn't matter if you consented. It would be unlawful of him to have carnal knowledge of you in Louisiana."

She shrugged.

"Anything else you can add to describe this man?"

"Harrell smells like the seashore. The other man had real hard skinny fingers. He kept saying, "Sweet Mary, sweet Mary," when he was coming."

"Well."

"Not much help, huh?"

"What exactly does it mean to smell like the seashore?"

"Fresh, salty, I guess. I'm sorry. I'm a musician. I write country songs. It's just the way I talk."

"You sometimes dance professionally and you sing country songs?"

"Yes, I do."

"Anything else you remember?"

"When the other man was getting dressed, I saw a pin on his shirt that said FROG on it."

"What's that mean?"

"I don't know. Maybe a club, I thought. Maybe that's his name. He was a frog, as far as I was concerned."

"You ever see either one of them since that time?"

"No, but that same personals ad is back in the paper this morning."

4

It was no big surprise that Judge Al Hughes called Tubby Dubonnet at home. After all, they had been friends for twenty years. Tubby had recently concluded his reign as cochairman of the Hughes reelection campaign. The surprising thing was the fear in the judge's voice.

"I've got a problem, Tubby. Have you got some time? I would like to discuss it with you right away."

"Of course I've got time. How big a problem is it?"

"Big enough. When can we meet?"

"Right now if you want. I could be down at your office in half an hour."

"I'm not sure how private that is. What about your house?"

"Okay with me. It's a mess, but you know the way."

"I'm leaving in a few minutes," Hughes said, and hung up.

Within half an hour the judge—portly and elegant—was sitting at the round table in Tubby's kitchen. The dishwasher was humming from a last-minute cleanup job, and Tubby was putting CDM coffee into the pot.

"I'd offer you a beer, Al, but I haven't got any."

"That's not like you. Getting in shape for a pool party?" the judge asked, making a small attempt at humor, but the twinkle was missing in his eye.

"Coffee it is, then," Tubby said, looking around for napkins.

"Forget it. Just listen to me for a few minutes."

"Roger, chief." Tubby sat down. He had never seen Al Hughes this distressed, and he feared he was about to hear about a terrifying medical diagnosis.

"I've been a judge for fourteen years," Hughes said. "I've made some good calls and some bad calls, but I always could face myself in the mirror. Now I . . ." He choked. "The bastards are out to get me," he said, showing his teeth.

"Which bastards, Al? What are you taking about?"

"The goody-goodies, son. The holier-than-thous. To name names, Marcus Dementhe, our extremely repressed and rapacious district attorney."

"Marcus Dementhe?" That was bad news. The celebrated race in the recent election had not been for judge but for district attorney. Dementhe was the new man in, succeeding the crusty old Boy Scout who had retired after holding the job for a couple of generations. In victory Marcus Dementhe was arrogant. Tubby thought him a bitter, crafty person. His literature said he went to

church every Sunday. In protest Tubby had voted for
Yvette Pews, who got her customary twenty-six percent.

"Yeah, the prick." Hughes looked around nervously. "Anybody else here but you?"

"I wish," Tubby said. "No, I'm here alone. I have a
temporary boarder, but he went down to the newspaper
for some reason."

"No girlfriends, huh?"

"It's been a bad year."

"For me, too, it looks like. I'm under investigation."

"What in the world for?" Hughes was straight as an
arrow.

"For having a relationship with a woman other than
my wife."

"You?" He was dismayed. Recovering, he said,
"That's not illegal in Louisiana, except in the most technical sense, of course."

"This is pretty damn technical, I can assure you.
The point, however, does not seem to be to put me in jail
but to humiliate me and threaten me into cooperating
with a full-blown investigation of what our new DA perceives as corruption in our local judiciary."

"Wait a second. Better start at the beginning."

"It's quite embarrassing talking to you like this, but
I am forced to conclude that I do need a lawyer."

"Well, sure."

"And this doesn't go any further than you."

"Of course."

"There's this girl. Let's call her Peggy Sue. She has

apparently told the DA that she and I had sex in my chambers at the courthouse.''

"I see."

"That I touched her genitalia," Hughes said dryly. "That's the way Dementhe put it. He summoned me to his office with a telephone call. He mentioned the young lady's name, and I couldn't say no. I had to actually postpone a trial in progress for the first time in my career."

"You went alone?"

"Yep. I should have called you first, but I was in shock, I guess. He made me wait a half hour too. But we finally talked in his office—alone. He presented me with the dates, times, and places when he said I had sex with the girl. He said he's going to pull me before a special grand jury he's convening to nail corrupt judges. He said he might work out a deal with me if I cooperate with him by providing some dirt on my colleagues."

"Anyone in particular?"

"No. He mentioned Judge Trapani like it was a joke because that's a giveaway. Trapani already has his share of problems with the Judiciary Commission. He also mentioned Boggas and Tusa."

"Both of whom he opposed in the last election."

"Yeah. He's hated them for years."

"How are they supposed to be corrupt?"

"Hell if I know," Hughes said. "They don't tell me their secrets. Our DA may want me to manufacture something."

"What did you tell him?"

"That I had to think about it for a few days. Then I called you."

Tubby looked at his reflection in the toaster.

"Son of a bitch wouldn't shake my hand," Hughes muttered. That seemed to bother him as much as anything else.

"How much of the stuff about the girl is true?" Tubby asked, still looking at the toaster.

"Depends on what you mean by sexual relations."

"Come on, Al. You know that dog is dead."

"If any of this gets out, Tubby, my wife will leave me flat. No two ways about it. I can't have that."

"What do you want me to do, Al? Never screw a client, never lie to the judge—that's me. But you've got to lay it out now."

"I want you to represent me, for Chrissakes. Find out what they've got on me and make me the best deal you can. Better than I deserve, if possible."

"You messed up, huh?"

"Big time. I feel so damn sick about this, so guilty and disappointed in myself, I can barely sit here and talk about it."

"How did you meet the girl?"

"She was at a campaign party Lucky LaFrene put on for me at his house. I don't know who she was there with, but Lucky introduced us."

"Lucky LaFrene the car dealer?"

"That's him."

Tubby had never met the man, but he was a local celebrity, well known for TV ads where he threw money into the air and squealed, "Get Lucky at LaFrene's!"

* * *

Lucky LaFrene's immodest stucco mansion glowed with a thousand lights. Big shiny cars lined the curbs in both directions, and a mounted policeman at the corner exchanged pleasantries with well-dressed couples walking toward the party. His horse quietly sampled the St. Augustine lawn.

The front doors were wide open, and incoming guests could stop at a little table to fix a name tag for themselves. Some, trusting in their notoriety, stepped right into the vast great hall where congestion was developing around four well-distributed bars. Black men with frilly shirts and cummerbunds concocted the night's specials with never-dimming smiles.

There was no mistaking who the host was. Lucky LaFrene was recognizable to almost everyone who watched TV, and he was the loudest person in the room. Also, he was the only man with a bouffant hairdo wearing a pink tuxedo.

"Please don't give me no news from Washington," he begged one silver-haired lady in a pearly cocktail dress. *"They can all croak on their own venom. The only politics I care about are right here in New Orleans, darlin'."*

"Hey, sweetie." He grabbed the elbow of an attractive young brunette trying to slip past toward the hors d'oeuvres. *"You know, you could be on* Babe Watch.*"* She crossed her eyes at him. Lucky laughed and let her go.

"Where's the paparootzie with their cameras?"

LaFrene—known in used-car circles as the "great artic-ulator"—cried. "We've got some stars out tonight."

A tall man wearing a white linen suit and sunglasses came from the hall and entered the room. Behind him was a slight, coffee-colored woman in a blue sarong, gold bracelets on her wrists.

"My man, Finn!" LaFrene shouted when he spotted the new arrival. "Come on in and buy yourself a drink!"

Finn worked the crowd, shaking a few hands on his way to the center of the room.

"Nice turnout, Lucky," he said appreciatively. "I didn't know you had so many friends."

"What are you talkin' about? I've got more friends than China's got peas."

"Are they here to support your candidate for judge, or just for the food?"

"I done raised twenty-five thousand dollars," Lucky confided happily. "What nice contribution are you going to make?"

"What is Judge Al Hughes going to do for me? I don't get into trouble."

"It never hurts to know the man on the throne," Lucky said wisely.

"I'm just here to drink," Finn admitted.

"Then go get yourself a penis colossus. We're hav-ing a beach party. Speaking of which"—he put his lips by Finn's ear—"it's time we did the deal on your boat. You owe me, doodley, and I'm ready to ride."

Finn laughed. "I'll have your dough sometime next week," he said, and pushed off toward one of the bars.

"That story's got more holes than a Swiss watch," LaFrene said to no one in particular. *"Hey, here's the judge!"*

The four-piece combo known as the "Dixie Gentlemen" was just starting to play when Judge Hughes made his entrance. The lady with the pearly dress started foxtrotting to "I Remember Judy," which instantly created a space around her as nearby guests guarded their drinks and cheese straws.

Unawares, the judge stepped into the circle and waved to Lucky. He promptly found himself with a dance partner.

Not unaccustomed to the spotlight, he gave the jolly lady a spectacular twirl. Encouraged by much clapping, the judge was about to improvise a few tango moves when LaFrene came to his rescue.

"He can sidestep just like Fred MacMurray, folks!" the host yelled, grabbing Hughes's hand just as he was attempting a personal pirouette. *"Let me introduce Judge Alvin C. Hughes! My candidate for civil district court!"*

After a round of applause the candidate was guided to the nearest potential donor by Lucky LaFrene.

Miffed, the abandoned dancer drifted up to the band and tried to croon along with the banjo player.

The young woman in the blue sarong sat quietly on a sofa, munching a ham biscuit and watching the judge move around the room in her direction.

* * *

"She was quite flirtatious," Hughes continued, "and I suppose I found that flattering. She said something indicating she was very supportive of my campaign and wanted to help, and I made a big mistake. I told her she could come and talk to me about it anytime."

"And she did."

"They say there ain't no fool like an old fool."

"You're not that old."

"I sure feel old today."

"How often did she come to your office?"

"Two or three times."

"Which was it?"

"Three, to be specific, Counselor."

"That's the way it's got to be. Did anyone see her?"

"Sure. Mrs. Evans was there. She let her in the first time. The other times were during lunch, so I don't know. Maybe one of the clerks saw her."

"Did she actually do any work for the campaign?"

"Not much."

"How old is this woman?"

"About twenty-five, I'd say. I didn't ask to see her driver's license. Maybe she doesn't have one. She's East Indian."

"Did she have a wire on her? You know, a tape recorder?"

"It would have had to be a mighty small one."

"District Attorney Dementhe did not mention a wire?"

"No. He said that she had come to him anxious to confess the whole story and that she is cooperating fully."

"Why do you think she did that?"

"I've got to believe I was set up."

Tubby leaned back in his chair and closed his eyes. After a moment he rocked forward hard, making a loud thump.

"Okay. Here's what I want you to do," he said. "Go back to your job. Don't say anything about this to anyone else. If the press calls, don't call them back. If anyone sticks a microphone in front of you, say, 'I have a lawyer who handles all my personal questions,' and refer them to me. I'll go talk to Marcus Dementhe and see what he really wants. Do you know how I can get in touch with the girl?"

"I've got her phone number. What do you think I ought to tell Mrs. Hughes?"

"Jesus, Al. I don't have the slightest idea."

His friend stared hard at the tabletop.

"Maybe I shouldn't be a judge," he said quietly.

The lawyer kept his peace.

"What do you think?" Hughes asked weakly, wanting an answer.

"I think until we get a machine with a brain and a heart, judges are going to be people. I haven't met a perfect person yet, and that includes me."

"It means a lot to hear you say that."

"And before I forget, keep your conversations on the telephone to a minimum."

"Sure thing. Remember Judge Collins? He taught everybody that lesson."

"And as soon as possible, I'm going to send a private investigator named Sanre Fueres to check out your judicial chambers for listening devices. They call him Flowers. He's very good.''

''All right. So I wait to hear from you?''

''Yep.''

Hughes pushed back his chair and stood up, in a hurry to be gone. Tubby walked him to the front door.

''Nobody wants to show the whole world his backside,'' the judge said somberly.

''Yeah, but don't forget what Edwin Edwards said.''

''What's that?''

''The voters wouldn't care unless he got caught in bed with a live boy or a dead girl.''

''That was back when people had a sense of humor,'' the judge grumbled.

''True.''

''And he's likely to die in jail.''

''You're right. Bad comparison.''

''My main worry is Olivia Hughes.''

After he left, Tubby dialed Flowers's number from memory, but his thoughts were with his unexpected client. If he had been asked which friend of his would be most likely to commit an embarrassing personal peccadillo, Alvin C. Hughes would not even have made the list. Sexual exposés were now all the rage. Was Al so above it all that he didn't even know that?

''Flowers, I've got a job for you,'' he told the message service. ''Dust off your magic mystery box and call me.''

5

The music was "Ahab, the Arab," and Sapphire was imitating a python, winding herself around a brass fire pole, flicking her tongue, and swinging her hair to the beat. The men in the place all wore shirts with collars, and half of them had on ties. The only ones not watching the snake writhe and undulate were getting the private attention of a table dancer shaking her powdered crotch at their eye level.

Raisin paid his ten dollars at the door, stepped around the island loaded with prime rib and potatoes au gratin, and took a little table alone.

His waitress, monumental butt restrained by a purple thong, offered him a drink.

"Whiskey and water, honey," he shouted over the music. The club was dark as a movie theater, but he left his sunglasses on.

Even in the shadows, charged with sexual tension,

he could tell that the dancer onstage was the woman from the videotape.

She had not been so hard to find.

The music changed to "I Saw Her Face." Raisin could see her face despite the fake lashes, lip gloss, and gold eye makeup. Her gaze was stuck on a distant mountaintop, and her lips quietly counted the beat while the rest of her did the act. His eyes traveled down her body, which was to all intents and purposes naked and shaved smooth as a leather purse. She definitely demanded attention—must be her muscle tone. There was something fascinating, disabling, to a man about a naked woman dancing in a dark room under colored lights.

His drink came, and he paid with another ten.

"Keep the change," he said, and the waitress slipped the bill in her waist strap. There were lots more there to keep it company. She likes me, he thought. Raisin knew he had a little sex appeal. Tanned and leathery, wavy black hair and a gleam in his eye, he looked like a ranger blown in from Wyoming.

When Raisin turned back to the stage he was barely in time to catch a final fanny wiggle as his girl undulated into the mirrors.

She returned once to strut around the perimeter of the stage, accepting applause and cash from the men within reach. When the next dancer appeared, Sapphire stepped daintily offstage to make the rounds of the tables in the back.

From what Raisin could tell, she did okay. She plopped onto some guy's lap for a moment, then jumped up giggling from the joke he coughed into her ear. When she got to Raisin he held up a twenty.

"Table dance for the gentleman?" she inquired, raising her arms high and twirling like an ice skater. He pushed his money into her briefs.

"How about just sit and have a drink with me," he said.

"Okay, mister." She fell lightly upon a vinyl-covered chair. One of her ankles touched one of his, and he could smell her cinnamon perfume.

"My name's Raisin. I've seen you on a videotape, and I've been searching for you for a long time."

She looked at him like he'd popped out of a manhole and stopped weaving in time to the music.

"What kind of videotape?" she asked.

"I think maybe you were at a police station. You were talking about answering a personals ad. You had coffee with a guy, and he came on to you."

"That was a long time ago."

"Thirteen months and change," he said. "A friend down at the paper went through the back issues with me until we found the ad."

"It wasn't a police station," she said. "Mister."

"Where was it?"

She shrugged. "Why are we talking?"

"I guess because I'm crazy. There was just something about you, about your story, I don't know, I had to meet you."

"So now we meet."

"Sapphire Serena? That's your name now?"

"You got it." She smiled and stood up.

Hastily, Raisin produced another twenty. "Hey, where's my table dance?"

She squinted at him, but put out her palm.

"Or if you'd rather, just sit back down and talk to me for another five minutes."

"Three, tops," she said, and sat down, crossing her arms over her breasts. Raisin noticed that the bartender across the room was starting to pay attention.

"To make a long story short," he said, "I'm only slightly perverted. I'm not a stalker. I can beat you at tennis. I'm into dining and dancing and redheads. Can I walk you home?"

"It's against the rules, I'm happy to say."

"Let's break the rules. I'll be good. We could have coffee or a couple of drinks when you get off work. If you're hungry, I'll spring for a meal. No strings. What do you say?" He gave her his most engaging smile. It had won him a lot of hearts.

"Sorry," she said. "It's time for my act." With that she hopped up and threaded seductively around the tables and through a black door beside the stage.

Raisin settled back and watched Apple Ambrosia stimulate herself with a feather boa. When she was finally lying on her back in apparent exhaustion, legs languidly peddling the air, the whole stage began to rotate. As the supine stripper disappeared behind a curtain, Sapphire returned, now dressed like a rodeo cowgirl with plenty of sequins, and the music shifted into something heavy on fiddles.

She had two similarly sparkling backup dancers, and the men in the audience were initially startled at the change of tempo and extensive clothing. They came to attention, however, when the three women started high-stepping, and Sapphire launched into an impressionistic rendition of "I beg your pardon. I never promised you a rose garden" to the accompaniment of a self-propelled synthesizer.

It was quite a show. Cowgirl hats got tossed around and most of the sequins got peeled away. Sapphire hit a fair number of notes right and she even sang a song about a trip to the sea which she said she had composed herself. The set lasted about fifteen minutes and then the band, called the Lady Hi-Balls, rotated off the stage, tambourines banging away.

Raisin stood up and applauded enthusiastically. The three performers skipped out of the door and passed around their Stetsons for tips. He caught Sapphire's eye by waving at her and whistling loudly. She made like she might ignore him but then she sashayed over to his table and held out her hat with both hands.

"Your singing is tremendous," he said. "I'm your biggest fan. Give me a chance."

She squinched up one eye and looked him over with the other one.

"I'll consider it," she said, "but no funny stuff."

"Cross my heart, sweetheart. Hey, you can come just as you are."

He thought he had lost her then, since she was frowning when she spun away.

But she looked over her shoulder and said, "I get off at two and I go across the street to the Monkey Cage for a tequila sunrise. You can find me there."

Yes, I can, he thought, as he watched her gossamer hips slip off into the gloom.

It was about four-thirty in the morning when Tubby Dubonnet was awakened by the sounds of hilarity in front of his house. He put a pillow over his head, waiting for the annoyance to pass, but it didn't. In fact, it seemed to build toward a crescendo in his front yard. He stumbled to the window, rubbing the sleep from his eyes, and beheld in the beam of the floodlamp that protected his steps Raisin and some female staggering around like walruses. Apparently twisted past caring, Raisin was trying to locate the key Tubby had lent him. The woman was finding the search hysterical.

At last he produced his object and triumphantly fitted it into the lock.

The sounds of mirth moved inside. The homeowner heard them banging around in the kitchen, and he got as far as the top of the stairs, intending to shut the party down, before he changed his mind and returned to bed.

He crammed the pillow back over his ears. Still, he heard them sneaking up the stairs to the guest room, shooshing each other and giggling. This was the last straw. Tomorrow Raisin was out of here.

Either that or Tubby was.

* * *

Tubby called Anita Baxter, the real estate agent who had sold him his house. Her voice, when she answered the phone, was fuzzy, and Tubby realized she was somewhere in traffic.

"I'm doing seventy-five on the I-Ten, darlin'," she cackled. "It's a good time to talk." He could hear sirens in the background.

"Is there a cop after you?" he shouted.

"No, that's an ambulance trying to pass me. You don't have to scream. I can hear you just fine."

"I'm thinking about selling my house." He lowered his voice. "How much do you think I could get?"

"More than you might expect, honey. How much of a hurry are you in? I can bring by a contract tonight."

"Not that much, really. I'm just thinking about moving."

"I can find you a great deal."

"To the Northshore," he added.

"Well, well." She laughed. "Ditching the big city, huh?"

He could hear a semi grinding its gears.

"I'm just giving it some thought," he hedged. "A little place in the country wouldn't be so bad, would it?"

"Depends on what you like, sweetie. Personally I like nightlife, but that's just my preference. I handle some great listings on the Northshore too. We can find you that perfect spot. Do you want to raise horses?"

"Maybe. Who knows? I'm not giving up on New

Orleans, understand. I'm simply exploring some options."

"Sure, honey. It's like they say: 'Will the last person across the causeway please blow it up.' As soon as I get to my office I'll fax you some pretty pictures."

6

Tubby had never met the new district attorney, Marcus Dementhe. He used to see the old DA at Saints games, and even once in court, but the Dubonnets and the Dementhes moved in different circles. Dementhe had been a "legal analyst" for a popular talk show and a spokesman for a large organization opposed to underage drinking before the election, and despite the inherited wealth that bought him plenty of TV time he would not have won the job if his main opponents, Lefty Mannaheim and Harvey Hood, had not been such obvious hacks.

During his six months in office Dementhe had cleaned house and fired everybody above the level of file clerk. Thus, the faces of the earnest men and women bustling around the DA's office were new to Tubby. The pudgy receptionist was polite enough, however, when she told him to please have a seat. For the next thirty minutes he stared at a copy machine, until the DA gave her the signal.

"You're here on behalf of Judge Hughes." Marcus Dementhe was stating the obvious while examining the lawyer from head to toe. At six foot plus, Tubby usually looked down on people, but Dementhe stood a head taller. The other dissimilarity was that everything about Dementhe—from his beaklike nose to the long fingers that briefly touched Tubby's—was thin.

"This is my first assistant, Candy Canary." He indicated the woman standing quietly by a brown leather chair in the corner of the spacious office. In the shadows she would have been easily overlooked, but she had bright, glistening eyes.

"Won't you sit down," the DA offered magnanimously.

"Thank you. I appreciate your seeing me on such short notice."

"The Hughes matter is quite serious," the DA said, lowering himself softly behind his wide desk. Above his head was a painting of black flambeaux strutting in a Mardi Gras parade.

"Well, what exactly does the 'Hughes matter' encompass?" Tubby wished to keep the serve.

"Didn't he tell you about our meeting?"

"Of course. That's why I'm here."

"Then you know we have received credible evidence of malfeasance in office and violations of the Canons of Judicial Ethics, and I suspect a great deal more."

"What exactly is this evidence?"

"These are the ground rules. I'm not going to pussyfoot around with you, and I'm not going to argue with you. I will tell you the basis for our investigation, but not its extent. I have assigned my top people to this. Your client is but the tip of the iceberg."

"I wish I knew what you were talking about," Tubby said, furrowing his brow.

"Specifically, your client engaged in sex acts with a person over whom he held the power of the court. Give Mr. Dubonnet a sample of the details, Candy."

"Certainly, sir. On September eighteenth, Miss—" The DA slapped his desk, and she stopped abruptly.

"Let's not mention names," Dementhe said.

"Of course. On September eighteenth the informant entered Judge Hughes's private office. She was admitted by the judge's secretary, a Miss or Mrs. Evans, at approximately two-fourteen P.M., and she remained there until approximately two forty-two. During that time she asked the judge a number of personal questions relating to his preferences in women and what he liked to do for fun. On the pretext of explaining how she might fit in to his campaign organization, of which you, Mr. Dubonnet, were the cochairman, he likewise asked personal questions about her.

"She felt that the judge was attracted to her and was making advances to which she was not unreceptive. Upon her departure the judge held her hand for an inappropriately long time. He asked for, and was given, her personal telephone number."

The first assistant flipped a page in her notebook. Tubby, who had sunk guiltily in his chair when she mentioned his name, wished he had a notebook of his own.

"On September twenty-first," Candy continued, "Judge Hughes called Miss, uh, the informant at her home at six o'clock in the evening and invited her to come to his chambers on the following day. He suggested twelve-fifteen, at which time his staff would be gone for lunch—"

"He said that to her—that his staff would be out?" Tubby interrupted.

The first assistant regarded him bleakly. Apparently give-and-take was not to be a feature of this lecture.

"The informant arrived at the courthouse a few minutes after noon, as instructed. She took the elevator to the judge's floor and found the door to his chambers locked. She knocked, and the judge himself let her in. They walked into his chambers. No one else was present. As before, the judge began the interlude by talking about his campaign and what he said was his need to reach out to the youth vote, to get young people involved in the process. She reports that they were sitting together on his couch, that their hands and knees touched, and that suddenly she found herself in his arms."

Tubby rested his chin on his fist, hoping he was not blushing.

"At that time the judge became visibly aroused and fondled her breasts. He broke off the physical contact and told her she would have to go, which she did."

Thank God, the lawyer thought.

The first assistant continued. "On September twenty-fourth the judge again called the informant." Oh, no, Tubby said to himself. "He apologized for what had happened, though she explained that she believed it was her fault." The first assistant frowned. "The judge assured her that nothing like that would occur again, and she suggested that she would still want to work on his campaign. He invited her to come to his chambers again—again at lunchtime."

District Attorney Dementhe stared woodenly at Tubby, who felt properly skewered to his chair, and his first assistant adjusted her glasses and continued.

"On September twenty-fifth the informant again knocked on the door of Judge Hughes's courtroom, arriving at twelve thirty-three. On this occasion she stayed for approximately thirty-five minutes. They again sat on the couch, and after conversing for a short time, they again began touching each other. They embraced, and the judge helped her unbutton her blouse. He felt her breasts and underneath her skirt. She undid his belt and his zipper, exposing the judge's penis. He achieved orgasm with her sitting on top of him."

"With her sitting on top?" Tubby demanded.

"Why, yes," Ms. Canary said.

"What does that have to do with anything? What is all this detail for? Is there any connection between these alleged events and any of the duties of the judge's office? Was the woman a litigant in his court?"

Marcus Dementhe's face became animated for the first time. He positively glowed.

Miss Canary nodded her head vigorously.

"Yes, sir," she said. "Three years ago the informant was cited for contempt of court for failing to obey a restraining order to stay away from an individual, and an attachment was issued for her."

Tubby's heart sank, and an unpleasant pain poked him in the stomach.

"The judge who signed the attachment was Alvin Hughes. The young lady was subject to being arrested at any time and taken to jail."

"That's ridiculous," Tubby said hotly, thinking just the opposite. "The judge probably signs a hundred orders a day. You're talking about an old case that's probably been disposed of long ago. There's no illegality here. That's hardly even an impropriety."

Dementhe's voice displayed no doubt when he said, "I'm afraid we have reached a different conclusion, Mr. Dubonnet. You see, we think that our informant may have hoped to influence the judge to erase the attachment and that he took advantage of her vulnerability to obtain sexual favors."

"Has he confirmed any such thing?" Tubby inquired indignantly.

"No, he has not," the DA conceded, and here for the first time Tubby thought there might be a ray of hope. "But the facts speak very plainly. To deny those facts would be to risk committing perjury or, worse, obstruction of justice."

The lawyer started to protest again, but thought better of it.

"Well, sir," he began more contritely, "you have been good enough to share this much of your case with me. Now tell me what your plans are."

Dementhe leaned back and made a steeple with his fingertips.

"It is becoming clear," he said, "that some of the

civil and criminal judges of the parish are in fact criminals themselves. The sale and barter of reduced sentences, or no sentences at all, for the parasites of our society has reached a nadir of contemptuousness. Bribery has become a way of doing business. Judge Hughes is but one sad example. His sordid practices we cannot ignore, but we can discount them. As for the others, they are joined in a conspiracy to thwart the justice system, and they must pay in full. To the extent that Judge Hughes can help us identify and expose these acts of public corruption, we will consider that cooperation when deciding how severely to prosecute him.''

''What sort of cooperation are you talking about?''

''Who's to say? First he should be forthcoming with us about his own misdeeds, then about those of his colleagues. Then we'll see.''

Ms. Canary piped up, ''He could be asked to record conversations with certain other judges, or put over a sting.''

''What if he doesn't know anything?'' Tubby asked.

''Then society will be better off with him in jail,'' Dementhe said evenly.

''And if he does cooperate, what is his reward?''

''Other than virtue?'' Dementhe chuckled. ''He would not go to jail unless, naturally, there are other indiscretions we do not yet know about. He would, in any event, be required to resign from the bench.''

''Resign his judgeship?''

''Of course,'' Dementhe and Canary said together.

''Over a family matter?''

''That's an interesting concept,'' Dementhe said reflectively. "A man who would betray his family, and the very institution of the family, cloaking his behavior in the mantle of family privacy. Tut-tut, Mr. Dubonnet, that just won't do."

"We all know that families aren't perfect," Tubby argued. "That's why they need privacy."

"Including yours, isn't that right, Counselor? Even including yours."

"What in the world are you speaking of?" Tubby was incredulous.

"Why, your own daughter and her extramarital affairs."

The lawyer's face colored like a muscadine. "Are you crazy? Have you got me mixed up with somebody else?"

"And didn't she check herself into some sort of halfway house," Dementhe pressed, "—a so-called church mission, in Mississippi? And didn't she there require counseling on this very subject?"

Tubby was speechless for once in his life. This man was threatening him, and he did not even know what the threat was about.

Numb, he stood up and turned toward the door, shaking his head to try to clear it. Mr. Dementhe and Ms. Canary watched his departure in sober silence.

Tubby was still in a daze when he walked out of the building into the bright sunshine on Tulane Avenue. A beggar tossing peanut shells at a horde of shuffling pigeons scowled at him from a bus stop bench. The lawyer sat down next to the man. He waved his foot to keep a bird from pecking on it, and he put his head to work.

The reference to his daughter's extramarital affairs had to be to his oldest girl, Debbie, who had been about five months pregnant when she walked down the aisle last summer. He prayed the DA was not talking about Debbie's younger sisters. The wedding had resolved the issue of her pregnancy, most people would agree, so all Tubby could figure was that the DA, in his zeal to crucify everybody, had missed the fact that there had been a ceremony. And, yes, Debbie did have a connection with a church-type outfit over in Bay St. Louis, Mississippi, so it must be her. Tubby was vague about the details, but Debbie had asked the head man of the place, the Reverend Buddy Holly, to read the vows in her wedding. The Dubonnets' old church pastor had generously agreed to share his pulpit, and everything had gone off without a hitch. So what was so suspicious about that? How would Marcus Dementhe know about Buddy Holly's little mission?

There was another angle here, too, if you were truly paranoid. Tubby had been quietly fantasizing about Buddy Holly's chief-cook-and-bottle-washer, Faye Sylvester, for the past month. It had begun like this.

7

Tubby's new self-improvement regimen involved more than staying off the bottle. He had also started playing softball on Saturday mornings. It was basically a church and bar league, and coed, which was why they sometimes let Tubby play. He had met Faye when the season was three games old. At that time he had yet to get a hit. It did not matter. Dressed in cutoffs and a couple of mismatched T-shirts, he was happy sitting on the bench cheering for the guys who actually had some ability. Just one more step toward a cleaner, more positive lifestyle, he told himself, watching the Gulf Coast Lost Sheep, a ragtag assortment of sexes and ages, warm up on the field. His own team didn't even have a name, so far as he knew.

Something about the sandy-haired pitcher for the Lost Sheep had struck him as familiar, and Tubby craned his neck to study the fellow better. Sure, it was the Reverend Buddy Holly, half of the minister duo who had performed the wedding for Tubby's daughter. At that time he knew only that Holly ran some sort of mission for misguided youth near Bay St. Louis, Mississippi, fifty miles away.

"Howya doin', Reverend?" Tubby yelled, poking his nose through the wire mesh backstop.

The young preacher recognized the lawyer, despite his bright, out-of-uniform attire, and waved back. After a couple more practice pitches he trotted over to the fence and they shook hands.

"Nice to see you, Mr. Dubonnet," he said, socking his glove. "I didn't know you played softball."

"In a manner of speaking, Pastor. You guys sure traveled a long way for this game."

"It's just an excuse to get to New Orleans. We all go out to lunch afterwards. Some of the girls like to go shopping, you know. . . ."

Tubby didn't hear the rest of the reverend's sentence. Walking toward them on the third-base path was a gangling, touchingly awkward woman about five foot nine with short black hair, outfitted in blue shorts and a crisp white T-shirt, who reminded Tubby of a lost puppy and, better, an old flame from high school.

Her aura of helplessness was quickly dispelled when she cried, "You want me to bat leadoff or cleanup today?"

While her captain considered, she said, "You're Tubby Dubonnet, right?" Her drawl was thick with syrup.

"Sure," he replied, flattered. "How did you know?"

"Oh, somebody mentioned your name to me. And I remembered reading about your victories in the Sonny Dan case and, what's the name of the man they tried to nail for beheading one of the doctors at the Moskowitz Memorial Labs?"

"Cletus Busters," he admitted, puffing out his chest. "I had a lot of luck in both of those trials."

"I'd like to hear about it sometime," she said. "Do you want me to play in the field, Buddy?"

Close up, Tubby could see that his fan was truthfully no spring chicken, but she had made a very favorable first impression.

"I'm going to have you start in center," Buddy told her.

The woman—Tubby guessed she was about thirty—tapped the brim of her cap with two fingers and gave Tubby a nod.

"The sun sure is hot, huh?" she said in parting, and trotted back to her bench.

"Nice lady," Holly said. "And single too."

"Yeah?" Tubby had found himself oddly smitten by this woman. He gradually let his stomach back out.

"She's been staying at our church for the last couple of months. She cooks for the kids."

"What kids?" he asked, concerned.

"Runaways, mostly. We've got bunks for ten and a lot of floor space, and we usually stay full. We try to clean up a few of the problems caused by our special combination of beaches, dockside gambling, and too much plain-old Mississippi. Didn't Debbie tell you about our mission?"

Tubby had never thought to talk to his daughter about it. "How did she, uh, meet you, Buddy?" he asked.

"She just drifted in," the preacher said vaguely. "You should talk to her about it sometime."

"I will." It was frightening what parents did not know about their children's lives.

"Turn in your rosters if you're playing!" the umpire cried from his seat in the bleachers.

Tubby failed to bring up the subject with his daughter.

Tubby's team was trailing six to zip in the bottom of the seventh inning, so his captain, Square Botts, had finally told him to pick up a bat. By that time his neck was sore from stretching and twisting to keep the center fielder in view. Despite being all elbows she had caught most of the pop flies that had come her way. She also had one hell of an arm, and once she got her grip on a ball she could peg it all the way home.

With visions of knocking one over her head and out of the park, Tubby took the first pitch. He felt a bit dizzy from the excitement.

"Strike one!" the umpire yelled.

He could almost feel the high fives his teammates would give him when he tagged the home run.

"Strike two!"

He was going to swing at the next pitch unless it was three feet over his head.

Buddy floated one right over the plate, and Tubby

connected with all of his convictions. Like a seventeen-year-old he pounded up the base path.

The ball sailed high—so high that it was still up there when the slugger rounded first. The shortstop backed up; the center fielder ran in.

"I got it, I got it," Faye cried, and she did. With a solid thunk the ball landed in her glove just as Tubby thundered to second.

"Great catch!" he called happily, panting, lingering, pandering.

"Nice hit," she called back, wiping sweat from her brow. She smiled.

"How about lunch?" he suggested.

She waved and ran back to her position.

"Batter up!" an umpire yelled, reminding Tubby where he was. He loped back to the bench.

Tubby caught up to her after the game and renewed the invitation. Why he liked her, he wasn't quite sure. Maybe because she was not exactly pretty. Maybe because when he smiled she smiled back.

"Want a bite to eat?" he asked, not very elegantly.

"I'm with the gang." She indicated her teammates, who were rounding up gloves and balls and drinking victory sodas.

"The plan is to shop at the Riverwalk and eat before we head back," Buddy Holly informed them as he walked by.

"You could catch up with your crew there in two hours, easy," Tubby said.

"We're sweaty," she pointed out.

"Not a problem." Tubby laughed. He knew lots of great places where nobody would mind.

He ended up taking her to Liuzza's by the Track, and they had cups of andouille gumbo with four shrimp and two oysters each for appetizers. A couple of young women from Kentucky came in to celebrate winning some money at the Fairgrounds. They had already kicked their shoes off and were talking loudly in accents clearly Southern, so Faye, in her MISSISSIPPI—A LAID-BACK STATE T-shirt, must have felt quite at home.

She ordered barbecued shrimp, which she said she had never had before. The waitress pleased her by tying a plastic bib around her neck so she would not get spots on her clothes. Tubby ordered baked garlic oysters.

By the time they had finished their soup, Faye had learned about Tubby's divorce and the names and ages of his children.

By the time he was sliding a fork under his first baked oyster, careful not to prick its tender surface, he had found out that her job as den mother for Buddy Holly's bad boys and girls was in the nature of a retreat from the demands of the real world. She was apparently recovering from troubles of her own, and for her the Mississippi countryside was the place to do so.

She had a few bad things to say about New Orleans: "Crime—stuff like that," she said.

They inadvertently touched feet under the table. He looked up from his plate long enough to see on the television hanging by the bar a replay of Mark McGwire hitting his sixty-first home run to top Roger Maris.

In a happy mood, Tubby ordered bread pudding for dessert. It came topped with whipped cream from a can.

Conversation was secondary but successful. A few meaningful personal details were exchanged between satisfied murmurs. In short, they got along.

Tubby ran her back downtown to meet her teammates and asked if she would like to get together again sometime. Sure, she said, and they left it at that. The topic of his daughter Debbie never came up then either.

8

Lucky LaFrene was having a great time rolling dice at the Casino Grand Mal, but his buddy, Max Finn, was all the way into outer space.

"Eeeaat Me!" Finn screamed, face flushed, eyes fiery, when he pitched his ivory cubes down the table. A ring of chattering, hopped-up guys and dolls egged him on.

"Point," the croupier said to cheers and laughter. The security man with his coat and tie watched without expression. He was used to Max Finn, the wild bunch that collected around him, and the noise they needed to make to have fun.

Finn grabbed his eighth Jack Daniel's and Diet Pepsi and gargled it. "Eyee!" he cried to the cameras on the ceiling. He rubbed the dice between his palms like prayer beads.

A showgirl with shiny white hair and a low-cut

cocktail dress kissed him on the mouth for luck, and
Finn swatted her rump.

Repeating his war cry, he flung the dice again.

"Point!" the croupier intoned, and cheers erupted.

"He's got the Morgus touch," LaFrene, a master of
miscommunication, shouted into the blonde's ear, and
she cackled merrily at his malapropism.

Finn threw handfuls of chips at the croupier and his
troupe of friends and swept the rest into his coat pockets
and his lady's handbag. He put an arm around her so far
that he cupped a dazzling jewel-encrusted breast in his
hand and jerked her back from the table.

"Magnifico!" he blared to anyone who was listening, barging through the crowd with the woman in tow.
He reached for a drink off a passing tray but missed.

"Ain't life grand," Lucky LaFrene proclaimed, trying to keep up.

Finn stumbled into the last row of slot machines by
the wall and fell against the woman, pressing her back
against 777 DEVIL'S DELIGHT. He stuck his tongue between
her wet lips and she tried to swallow it. His fingers
pulled her tight dress up her thighs, and she pushed a
hand down his pants.

Lucky LaFrene found them.

"About that money you owe me, Max," he began.
"Jeez oh flip!" he cried. "You'll get us all exhumed."

Telling Raisin to get out was easier than Tubby had expected.

He caught his disheveled but winsome guest with

his head stuck in the refrigerator searching for more bottles of beer, and the words just popped out.

"It's been fun, Raisin, but the time has come for you to move on."

"How much time do I have?" The vagrant dug out a Bud and straightened up. The cap twisted off easily.

"How does a day or two sound?"

Raisin stuck out his chin and took a swig. "No problem. Maybe I can hang out at Sapphire's until something else opens up."

"What's with that, man? She's young enough to be your daughter."

"It ain't quite that bad, buddy," Raisin said, cocking his head. "I don't have a daughter. And she's old enough to know what she's doing. Why don't you say what's on your mind?"

"It's your business." Tubby turned away.

"I guess so."

"You like her?"

"So far it feels okay."

"And you don't see a problem?"

"No. I get hornier every year because a broader range of women appeal to me."

"Meaning you see the beauty in older women."

"And younger ones. Listen, I'm not blind to the differences. I admit that even I think a twenty-year spread is extreme. Maybe it won't last. But she's been around a lot in her life. I had been, too, when I was her age." Raisin stopped, looking for understanding. He swallowed some more beer.

"It's your life" was all Tubby would give him.

"I know that. But before you get too superior, think about this. The women in my life, even the ones who dumped me, would tell you they don't regret the experience."

"Big deal."

"Well, would the ladies in your life say that?"

"I don't know. I just know I need to get some sleep around here, and it's gotten too crowded."

"Don't worry, buddy. I'm gone."

I'm getting my life in order, Tubby thought. He grabbed a can of Diet 7-Up from the refrigerator and angrily ripped off the top.

His lovely, wide-eyed secretary, Cherrylynn, rapped once on the door on her way to hand him some telephone messages. She was a little sour this morning because he had mentioned that she was late. It was true that Cherrylynn was competent at her job and had carried the ball for him a time or two when Tubby had been out of sorts, but if he could get to work on time, why couldn't she?

"I'm sorry, Mr. Dubonnet, but I'm going to be leaving at the end of the month." Cherrylynn's brave eyes didn't blink.

"You're quitting?" He was astonished.

"Yes, sir, and I'm giving you thirty days notice. Of course, if you don't want me to stay around that long, I'll understand."

"Well, I don't understand. After all these years. I didn't know there was a problem."

"It's not the same around here anymore," she said.

"It used to be fun. Now it just seems like a lot of pressure. I don't feel that you have appreciated my work, and I haven't been looking forward to coming here in the mornings."

"I don't know what to say." He stood up from his desk and almost went to put an arm around her shoulder when something in her expression made him stop. "Is it the money?"

"No, sir." She was adamant.

"Please stop calling me 'sir.' Have you got a better job?"

"I have my resumé out," she said grimly. "My plan is to take some time off and go to Cancún with a friend of mine."

"This is all so unexpected." He spread his hands in supplication. "Where would I get somebody to replace you?"

"I don't know," she said, almost crying now. "It won't be easy."

She abruptly turned on her heel and left the room. Tubby stared at the empty space. He felt lost.

It was not so difficult to locate the woman who had set Al Hughes up. The judge had given him the phone number and the name he knew her by, Sultana Patel. A woman's recorded voice, in an accent almost British, answered the phone, and Tubby left a message. She called back right away.

"You say you're Alvin's lawyer?"

"That's right, and it's important that I talk to you."

"Can I come over to see you right now? I'm feeling a lot of pressure here."

It must be going around, Tubby thought, and gave her the address. He told Cherrylynn to be on the lookout and asked very politely if she would mind staying in the room while he interviewed the woman.

"As of today you're a paralegal," he told her. "Anything you hear is privileged."

"Does that involve a raise?" she asked woodenly.

"Does it feel like Christmas?" She didn't smile, but he thought she might be brightening up a bit.

Sultana Patel showed up within thirty minutes. She did not look at all the way Tubby had pictured her. With a loose brown dress hanging from her skinny shoulders and her jet-black hair pulled back in a bun, she looked like a schoolmarm or a graduate student in art history. Her handshake was polite and her demeanor, while not exactly timid, was closer to a librarian's than a brazen hussy's. Something about her also conveyed a great weariness.

"Thank you for coming," Tubby found himself saying, and he offered her a chair. "This is my legal assistant, Cherrylynn, and I have asked her to join us."

Sultana nodded and swept her dress underneath her as she slid into the red leather chair. She crossed her hands in her lap and turned her large eyes upon the attorney. It seemed as though she was having trouble breathing.

"Hmmph," he began. "Well, we have a fine mess here."

"That's surely the truth," she said.

"I understand that you have been interviewed at length by the district attorney, and that you have testified before a grand jury."

"Yes," she admitted sadly.

"And in that statement you accused Judge Hughes of certain sex acts."

"I accused? They did all the accusing. I was threatened with going to jail and being deported. All I did was admit what they already knew, because I couldn't lie."

"Really? Well, let me start over. What is the truth?"

"The truth is that Alvin and I had some very special moments together, and they would have remained private between us except that somehow these investigators or whatever they are found out about it. I was having lunch with my girlfriend at the mall where I work and this man and woman came right up to my table and said they wanted to talk to me.

" 'What about?' I asked, and they got real nasty and showed me some identification, and my girlfriend got scared and she left, and I tried to leave, too, but they walked right along with me."

"Who were they?"

"I never got the man's name, but the woman was Candy Canary. She's the one who asked me all the questions later when they got me in the room."

"This lunch you're speaking about, this was the first time you met them?"

"Yes, and they claimed to know all about me and the judge, and that I had to talk to them at their office. I said I wanted a lawyer, and they said all right, but if I talked to them now I would be rewarded for my coopera-

tion, but they were under time constraints. If I got a
lawyer involved, that would slow everything up, and they
wouldn't be able to give me much of a reward.''

"So you talked to them."

"I started arguing, right? I'm sure I made a real
scene. I said I wanted to talk to some of my friends
first—"

"Let me guess," Tubby interrupted. "And they said
a twenty-four-year-old girl shouldn't need somebody to
hold her hand." He had the distinct feeling he had been
down this road before.

"That's right. They said that I had better go with
them right there or I would be getting into real trouble.
Both of them seemed so deadly serious, and of course I
was embarrassed and scared, so I just cried.''

"But eventually you went with them."

"Yes, I did eventually because I was frightened and
because I thought what Alvin and I had done wasn't
really very bad, and maybe I could make them see that.
Then they would leave us both alone.''

"Are you saying that you thought you might make
things easier for the judge by talking?"

She nodded. "I really care for the man.''

Tubby looked her over carefully. She met his eyes,
then looked down. Cherrylynn, who was taking notes
furiously, shot her a look.

"Where did you go for your conversation?'' he
asked.

"We got in this car they had parked right out by the
front entrance and drove to an office somewhere, the
district attorney's office. That's where we went.''

"Was Mr. Dementhe, the DA, there?"

"He came into the room after it was all over and just looked at me. He didn't say anything. He just looked at me. Then he left. Then they made me wait until my statement was all typed up, and I signed it. After that they let me go."

"You never had a lawyer present?"

"Not unless you call them lawyers."

"I mean, a lawyer on your side."

"No. I should have, I suppose."

"Okay. Back at the beginning, how did you meet the judge?"

"At a party they were having for the election," she said faintly. "It was at Mr. Lucky LaFrene's house."

"How did you happen to go to that party?"

"Well . . ." She hesitated. "Here's something I didn't tell them because nobody asked me. It's the most embarrassing part of all, and I never did tell Alvin."

Tubby beckoned with his fingers, meaning give it to me.

"I went there because a man asked me to. You see, I was in a sort of escort service."

"What's that mean?"

"This is very cheap sounding, but I had been in-volved with a man I met through, of all things, a newspa-per ad. You know, one of those personal ads? And after we got to know each other, you know, he said he could arrange for people to hire me for escorts to dinner or for parties or for things like that."

Why is this all sounding familiar? Tubby wondered.

"I needed the money, and he convinced me that all

of the men would be gentlemen. He said he would even pay me to go to the first party. That was the one where I met the judge. He told me that was who he wanted me to meet. He also mentioned that the judge was very lonely, and I should volunteer to be around him.''

''He paid you for this?''

''He did, after the party. He gave me one hundred dollars when I told him I had met Alvin and liked him, and that Alvin seemed to like me. He said I should keep up the good work and maybe I could make some more money. I know it sounds terrible, but things haven't been very good for me lately.''

''Were you asked to be a spy?''

''No, he never talked to me again after that, and he never gave me any more money. And I was glad, you see, because Alvin and I got our own thing going, and I wanted it just to stay that way.''

''Who was this man?''

''He told me his name was Harrell Hardy.''

''How could I find him?''

''I'm not sure. I never saw where he lives.''

''Was he by any chance tan, about six feet tall, black hair moussed up, dimple in his chin?''

''That's him,'' she said in surprise. ''Do you know him?''

''Just by reputation. Now I want to meet him in person.''

''I'm sorry. I wish I could help Alvin. I don't want to cause him any trouble. I'm just sick about the whole thing.''

"Uh, having intercourse is what caused him the trouble," Tubby said.

"Intercourse? Is that what Alvin told you?"

"You mean he didn't?"

"Actually, Alvin has this problem. . . ."

Tubby stood up fast. "Cherrylynn, you take over from here," he said, and he scooted out the door.

"What kind of perfume do you wear?" Cherrylynn asked. "I like it."

9

Bourbon Street rarely sleeps, but every morning it freshens up. Soon after the sun peeks over the slate roofs, bar sweeps with wide brooms and squeegees wash the booze off the floors and hose down the sidewalks until the gutters bubble with suds. Garbagemen dangling from moving trucks and speaking in strange tongues swoop down and swing black bags and tin cans of refuse into their machines' great maws, where it is compressed for shipment to distant pine barrens. Drunks get rousted from the stoops and alleys where they have fallen. The last of the revelers slip unsteadily back to their hotels, some pausing to compose themselves in doorways. White trucks venting jets of water bathe the street, sending whatever remains in a gurgling tide into the drains and on to Lake Pontchartrain and the sea.

Sapphire and Raisin were taking these moments to stroll hand in hand through the French Quarter. It was her favorite time of the day, when everything got clean again and before she headed back to her apartment to sleep it off and escape the day's heat.

Near the Old Absinthe House a man and a woman dressed for cocktails—he in a tuxedo and she in a slinky black dress—but both barefoot, crossed their path, arms entwined. They kissed deeply as they meandered and kissed again.

"Young lovers," said Sapphire, almost to herself.

Flinching inwardly at the word *young,* Raisin kept his mouth shut. He was dead tired and his feet ached, having picked his girl up from the strip club in the wee hours to spend what was left of the night drinking tequila with her and her pals. Now they were on their way to the Café du Monde for café-au-lait and beignets for breakfast. He would then sleep over at her place, but so what. He was wiped. The hours were killing him.

"I thought Ambrosia's dance was so, so, what's a good word, junglelike," Sapphire said. "Like a tigress. You know she really practices hard. And some nights she makes more than the rest of the girls combined. Doesn't that go to show that it's an art thing and not just boobs? I mean, we all have boobs, but the ones who do really well have some special talent."

"You've got something special," Raisin told her. He wasn't really listening but had an automatic pilot that beeped when a compliment was needed.

"Do you really think so?" she asked happily, and squeezed his hand. "Sometimes I don't think so. But I guess I've got something on the ball. Do you really think I have something special?"

"No doubt about it," he said, sidestepping the left-
overs of an oyster po' boy squished on the pavement.

"Then why won't you come and hear me play anymore?"

"I will if you really want me to. But I told you. I see
all the other men's eyes on your body, and it makes me
feel . . ."

"Jealous?"

"Well, not exactly. I suppose I want to be the only
one getting turned on when you're naked."

"Even though it's art?"

He looked at a cat running through a courtyard.

"That's cute, Raisin. I think it's cute that you would
be jealous."

She laughed. They walked quietly through the next
block, nodding at the shopkeepers and cooks on their
way to work, inhaling the temporarily moist clean air.

"Raisin, do you think we have a future?" she asked
when they turned the corner at Pat O'Brien's.

"Everybody has a future, honey."

She poked him in the ribs. "You know what I mean,
or are you being stupid on purpose?"

"I think it's too early to say exactly where we're
going," he tried again.

"I'm a girl in a hurry," she said, and let it drop.

Where I need to go in a hurry is to sleep, Raisin
thought to himself.

With Raisin evicted Tubby was finding it a bit lonesome
in his empty house. It was Friday. There was nothing he

wanted to see on television. He had finished reading about how "Huey Long Invades New Orleans," and he was happy to have someplace to go, even if it was a "Moonlight Serenade by Judge and Mrs. Alvin Hughes." This special treat was being held at the Royal Montpelier Hotel for the purpose of retiring the judge's campaign debts, and the tickets for the event were five hundred dollars a pop. Tubby had served as cochairman of the Hughes Campaign Committee, in which capacity he had managed to avoid actually having to donate any cash. Now that the judge had been elected, however, the invitation was hard to duck. He had examined his bank balance sadly and paid for two.

He thought maybe his daughter Debbie would go along.

"Have you forgotten what it's like, Daddy?" she demanded in exasperation. "I was up all night feeding Baby Bat. Marcos is crashed out in the living room from studying. I've got to fix supper tonight. I don't have anything in my closet that fits anymore. Except for that I'd love to go."

"It would be a nice break for you. Can't Marcos take care of the baby for a couple of hours?"

"Honestly, I'm just not up to it right now. My whole body is tired. Why don't you ask Mom? She likes those kinds of things."

"Debbie, your mother and I are divorced. That means we don't go out anymore."

"She'd probably say yes."

"Forget it."

"How about Collette or Christine? It would be educational for them."

"That's a good idea. By the way, is there any time in your busy schedule, like while the baby is asleep, when we could sit down and have a talk?"

"What about? Is something wrong?"

"No, no. I just feel like talking to you."

"Well, little Bat usually goes down for a nap at around ten in the morning."

"That would be good. Maybe I'll come over tomorrow."

"Okay. No guarantee that he'll sleep, though."

"How about if I bring some breakfast? Maybe some of those scones you like from the Daily Grind?"

"Oh, would you?" She was breathless with excitement. "We never go out anymore, and I'm absolutely starving for something that tastes really good."

Those are my genes, he thought proudly. They made a date.

Sultana concealed herself in the shadows cast by the shrubbery in front of the white-columned house. She had been fasting to cleanse her soul, and she was weak and light-headed. A slender tree by the driveway gave her some support. Seemingly wasting away, she was no bigger than a sapling herself.

Through the leaves above she watched black clouds wash in waves across a smiling moon, and she waited for his car to arrive.

Clutched under her shawl was a curved steel-bladed

knife with a brass handle. It had been her father's, and his father had worn it in a war. She was a shame to them all, and she would use this knife to take her own life. But she did not intend to die alone.

Christine did not answer the phone at her apartment. She was a freshman at Tulane now and was always hard to catch. Collette, however, still lived with her mother. He punched in the familiar number, prepared to hang up in a hurry if Mattie answered. She was on his case about extra money she thought he ought to contribute for harp-sichord lessons or something. On the first ring, however, his daughter picked up. She talked fast so as not to tie up her line with a nonessential call, and said it would be cool to go to the Serenade since, for some reason, she didn't have any other plans for the evening.

So Tubby arrived at the Royal Montpelier with his youngest daughter beside him in his blue LeBaron. She had on a dress that he had last seen her wear to her middle-school graduation party at Antoine's, and he noticed that she was starting to overflow it.

A turbaned valet wearing the khaki suit of a colonial magistrate offered in a Persian dialect to take the car away. The Dubonnets alighted into the muggy night.

"This sure is a fancy place," Collette said approvingly, holding up her gown so she wouldn't trip as they followed the red carpet up the marble steps. She returned a mujahideen's smile.

"Wait until you see the ballroom. A lot of famous people have performed there."

"Like who?"

"Well, let's see. The Drifters . . ." He got a blank look. "And Tina Turner." A flicker of recognition.

There was a crowd of politicians and well-dressed wellwishers in the palatial lobby.

Tubby shook a few hands and introduced his daughter around. His Honor himself was in the grand room at the epicenter of a loving swirl of people. He was laughing at jokes and slapping backs. One could not tell, looking at him, that he was living in fear of a grand jury indictment.

Tubby snagged some Cokes, and they waited their turn for an audience with the judge.

"Is this my main supporter?" Hughes cried, and parted some shoulders to grab a hand. "And who is this dazzling beauty? Collette? Looking fine, honey." He kissed the top of her head. "Anybody here not know Tubby Dubonnet, illustrious chairman of my reelection effort?" Tubby was mentally awarding the judge big points for acting ability.

"Glad to meetcha," said a red-faced man in a yellow suit. "My name's Lucky LaFrene, know what I mean?"

"You're the car salesman," Collette said, delighted. She liked anybody who was on television.

"That's right, my little pootsie. I've got more cars than dogs have bees, and every one of them's a steal. Let's do a deal."

"How do you do," she said, and giggled.

"I'm doing great. Judge Hughes is elected and all's right with my pearl. It's lovely to be with a winner. When are you gonna start singing, Judge? He's got a voice like Pepperoni," LaFrene promised.

At that moment there came a drumroll and Deon Percy, whom Tubby recognized as the Hughes campaign manager, hopped onto the stage and grabbed the microphone.

"The moment we've all been waiting for is here," he proclaimed amid screeches and whistles. "A tribute to a great man"—screech—"talents without equal"—whoooo—"now let me introduce Judge Hughes."

To enthusiastic applause Judge Hughes vaulted to the stage, bowed, and took a seat at the piano. He fiddled with the microphone, grinned at the audience, and broke into a rendition of "Hello, Dolly, this is Alvin, Dolly . . ."

Collette's eyes swept the room, absorbing details about how adults comport themselves. The judge's sister and some other campaign insiders began what appeared to be a mambo line. A barrage of balloons cascaded from the ceiling.

Tubby's gaze settled for a second upon Lucky LaFrene.

The colorful personality had moved to the side of the room and was bracketed by two guys with square shoulders in gray suits.

LaFrene was gesturing wildly, but he did not seem to be enjoying the music. His face was purple and his eyes were angry.

One of the men put a hand on him, and LaFrene

shook it off. The man put his hand back, and LaFrene left it there. A pained look spread over his face.

Despite himself Tubby started to move closer, for no reason but prurient curiosity. The altercation abruptly stopped.

"Hot-cha-cha, oh, baby, yeah." The judge signed off to thunderous applause.

"Dad, is this for real?" Collette wanted to know.

"I'm afraid so," he replied, and looked over her head. LaFrene had gotten lost in the crowd.

Mrs. Al Hughes jostled into Tubby, who, when he recognized her, planted a kiss on her cheek.

"We're so glad you're here," she said, and squeezed his hand.

"This is my daughter Collette. Olivia Hughes."

"So nice to meet you, dear. I hope you're having as much fun as I am."

"It's splendid," Collette said enthusiastically. "Very chic."

"I'm so glad you think so." The hostess's eyes sparkled. "You're a good girl."

She patted Collette, too, and continued on her errand.

"Oh, cool! Now they've got a conga drummer." Collette stood on tiptoes. "How seventies can you get?"

When Tubby looked to see what Olivia Hughes had pressed into the hollow of his hand, he found a small plastic horseshoe—a campaign token. He knew the slogan by heart: "Hey, Pal. Vote for Al. A Man You Can Trust."

"Oh, man," he complained.

* * *

Tubby dropped his daughter off at his old house and watched her run up the walk. It had been a really nice evening, he thought. He almost called out to her. She waved at the door and was gone.

Not many blocks away Sultana watched the car lights slowly approach on the quiet street. She edged farther into the shadows of the bushes when the car swerved into the driveway, and she tightened her grip on the long knife.

The car rolled past her and she saw that awful tall man behind the wheel. It rolled to a stop fifteen feet away. When the door opened and the man started to get out, she rushed from cover.

''You violated me,'' she cried, brandishing her knife. Surprised, the man fell back into the driver's seat.

He raised his arms to protect himself from the blade glinting in the streetlamp, but he was not the one she intended to kill.

With a defiant grunt Sultana brought the knife down and drew it across her own throat. Strangling, she fell into the car on top of the man.

Blood spurted over him as in horror he struggled to free himself from a tangle of arms and hair. He pushed her away with such violence that she landed on the lawn in a heap. He stood above her panting, covered in blood, wondering what his neighbors might have seen.

* * *

It had been a great evening, but driving home Tubby couldn't shake the fact that he was on his own again.

There had been women in his life, of course, since his divorce. There had been a misguided affair with Jynx Margolis, best described as the flashy ex-wife of a rich gynecologist. There had also been a short but promising relationship with Marguerite Patino, a rather larcenous tourist from Chicago, but he had no idea where she was today. And his current prospect was Faye Sylvester.

In the weeks following the softball game he had searched high and low for an excuse to visit Buddy Holly's mission, just to see her. He had found it two weeks before when, out of the blue, the phone rang and it was Mandino Fernandez, a client who owed him more than twenty thousand dollars in legal fees for success-fully resisting a foreclosure on Mandy's mother's home in the Garden District. The case was complicated, but Mandy's reason for not paying was simple. He was a spoiled brat. A charming spoiled brat. Tubby figured he would eventually have to sue the guy to get paid, which was a major pain in the neck, so he was immediately aroused when the first words he heard on the phone were "I've got your money."

"Bless you, my son. Where are you? I'll come get it." Such haste might be unseemly, but this was busi-ness.

"I'm killing the blackjack tables at the Coconut Ca-sino." He wanted Tubby to share in his good news.

"Come on over and join me for a few drinks. I'll flip you high card, double or nothing."

"I'm gone for the day," he called to Cherrylynn as he raced out the door. No time to mess around. He'd take his pay in chips—same as cash.

Tubby covered the seventy-five miles to Bay St. Louis in less than fifty-five minutes.

The cruise gave him a chance to go over in his mind the advantages he might enjoy by moving to the suburbs versus the disadvantages of commuting. There would be peace and quiet on the Northshore, and low crime, of course, though honestly the noise of trains and ships and a little big-city tension had never bothered him much before. There were pine trees and acre lots, too, but the main thing he imagined was clean living. He might have to get through another forty or fifty years of life, after all, and that would be better with pink lungs and liver and the kind of serenity a country person enjoys. He would be an hour away from his only grandson, little Bat, but maybe he could entice Debbie and Marcos to migrate north with him. Abita Springs, or Folsom, maybe, would be good places for a little boy to grow up, what with public schools and everything.

Before he knew it, he was breezing into the vast parking lot of the Coconut Casino, now the principal landmark of a once-sleepy town by the Gulf of Mexico. The casino itself was in an estuary, miles from open water. Since only "dockside" gambling was legal in Mississippi, the monumental structure technically floated, though it was locked firmly in place by concrete pilings.

He slid his blue LeBaron between a Winnebago from Oregon and a Jeep from Texas, and set off hiking toward the palatial front entrance. The last time he had been here was to watch his client, Denise Boudreaux, fight Roseanne Spratt, the Nashville Bomber, in the casino's boxing arena.

The security man nodded to him like an old friend, and Tubby was swept inside with the steady stream of gamblers arriving for action at the cocktail hour.

As soon as he entered the chilled lobby he spied Mandy sitting alone on a bench. But the pasty-faced man with the tousled hair seemed to sag, even as he stood up. He turned his palms skyward and displayed a forlorn expression. Tubby was too late. What the Lord had giveth, the Lord had already taketh back.

"All I've got left are two five-dollar chips," Mandy moaned. He fetched them from his pockets. "And I know you haven't got the heart to take those."

Tubby grabbed the red candies, took three steps, and fed them one at a time into a million-dollar payoff slot machine, which just as promptly ate them. The lawyer was too disgusted even to snag a free drink.

Roaring out of the parking lot, he decided on impulse to turn north toward where he figured Buddy Holly's mission was, thinking maybe he could salvage something from this trip.

The narrow blacktop quickly took him into a more pastoral environment. Neon gave way to brick ranch-style homes from the sixties, then mobile homes with pulpwood trucks in the front yard, and then fields occupied by solid black cows and realtors' signs. He braked hard when he spied a board nailed to a tree on which was painted CHAPEL BY THE BAY, with an arrow. A gravel road curved off into a field.

He crested a small rise and could glimpse, across a meadow overgrown with grass, blue water and white clouds.

"It's pretty out here," Tubby admitted to himself.

Almost blocking his path was a crooked billboard announcing that a Bayside Golf Community and Resort would one day occupy this acreage.

Tubby rolled down the windows and looked around, trying to imagine homes and streets rising from the woods and brambles. He couldn't.

The road snaked through what once might have been a pecan orchard, and then the bay suddenly appeared again across a wide marsh. The road turned to follow the shoreline and stopped at a ramshackle two-story farmhouse hugging a high spot of ground. A few old cars and a new van were scattered around the farmhouse yard.

Tubby parked in tall grass beside an old red Chevrolet with a sticker on its rusted bumper advising the world to DRINK NAKED.

Birds twittered in the branches of the cherry laurel tree by the front porch. Somewhere rock and roll music was playing, a door slammed, and there was distant laughter.

Tubby mounted the wooden steps.

He could see the narrow hallway dimly through the screen door. Tacked to the frame was a mezuzah and below that a cheap plastic plaque with the message JESUS WILL LIGHT OUR WAY. For some reason Tubby explored

them both with his fingertips before he pressed the
buzzer.

"Someone's up front!" a woman upstairs shouted.

"I'll get it," someone replied, and presently a
young man popped into the hallway and peered at Tubby
through the screen. He had bright blue eyes, a fuzzy
chin, and a T-shirt that said I'D RATHER BE MASTURBATING.
Tubby thought that was funny.

"Where'd you get your shirt?" he asked.

"In Florida. My girlfriend gave it to me," the boy
answered suspiciously.

"Really? Is Buddy Holly here?"

"He went to town." No move to open the door.

"What about Faye, uh, Ms. Sylvester? Is she
around?"

"Uh-huh. Who should I say is calling?"

Surprised at the politeness, Tubby gave his name and
sat down on the porch steps to wait. The boy slipped
away into the interior.

"Hello." Her voice made him jump.

"Oh, hi," Tubby said, getting up and brushing the
dust from his behind. "I was in the neighborhood."

"That's nice," she said. "Did Buddy forget you
were coming?"

"No. I didn't know myself." Tubby was losing himself in her eyes. They were green. "I mean, I didn't call
ahead. I'm just dropping in."

"I'm happy you did. Would you like to look
around?"

"Oh, sure. Buddy said to come over anytime. I was
down the road at the casino. Not gambling, of course. I

don't want to interrupt anything. Am I?'' He gave her his most hopeful expression.

Something about it struck her as funny.

"Come on in," she said, laughing. "I'll give you the cook's tour. After all, I'm the cook.''

With appreciation for the way she moved in blue jeans, he followed her into the hall.

"This is our formal dining room.'' She pointed through a plaster archway at a vast table. "That used to be in the boardroom of a bank that went out of business. We eat supper together every night. Right now there are twelve kids staying here, so with the staff we're feeding fifteen or sixteen.''

"Where is everybody?'' Tubby asked.

"School, work, shopping. We try to keep them busy.''

"Oh, excuse me,'' a vacant-eyed youngster said, barging into the hall and almost colliding with Faye. "I'm just going outside to smoke.'' She slipped quickly away and let the screen door slam behind her.

"Of course, not everybody is ready for the real world yet,'' Faye said wryly.

"Is this a church, a nuthouse, what?'' Tubby asked.

"A little of everything,'' she said. "Buddy can explain the religious side of things. He holds services every day. Some of the kids go. Some don't.''

"But what's the main point, I guess I'm asking.''

"Oh, you don't know that? These are all basically runaways. Buddy picks them up on Highway Ninety, hopefully before the police do or before they get too hooked on drugs.''

"What can you do for them?"

"Free room and board and a chance to chill out. You know, clean air, clean living."

Same thing I'm after, Tubby thought.

She asked him about his children, and he made some general comments—about them, about the divorce from his wife.

"Do you still see her?" she asked.

"Mattie? No. We get along better from a distance. She's got her own life and she's happy enough with it."

Faye showed him the grounds, and they took a walk along the sandy shore. She seemed a lot more relaxed out here than she had been in New Orleans. He learned that she had been married before, but she did not offer any details. She made some disparaging remarks about the Big Easy in general, with which he automatically agreed.

"It's so dirty, you couldn't clean it with Tide," she said. He thought she was talking about the litter but later wondered if maybe what she meant was the politics.

"It's so much better here," she said, "where you can breathe fresh air and smell the dew in the morning."

"Sure, that's nice," he agreed. "I've been thinking about moving out of New Orleans myself. You know, to the Northshore."

"That's not far enough, if you ask me. Louisiana just seems like such a hopeless mess. Mississippi is the place to be."

"Yeah?" He would have to pass a new bar exam to make a living here. Looking at the way her eyes crinkled when she smiled, he almost could believe it would be worth it.

"What are your plans for Thanksgiving?" she asked him.

"I don't know. It's kind of funny, with the kids all gone and all."

"We do a big meal here. You'd be welcome to come, of course."

"Yeah? Thanks. We'll see what happens."

"Country living is not so bad," she added, nudging his foot with hers.

He wanted to think that it was so, but with the moisture of the marsh creeping through his leather soles and the sun beginning to set behind violently crimson clouds he inexplicably had a cold sense of being out of place in this serene spot. The youngsters and their guardians were bonded together in ways that did not include him.

She invited him to stay for a communal supper of white beans and cheese toast, but to her surprise, he said he needed to get back to town. He made up something about a meeting. They shook hands smiling, said see you again, I hope, and Tubby drove away.

It had ended very awkwardly. Apparently he was not quite ready to be happy.

10

Cherrylynn dreamed up a plan, and then she made the bold decision to put it into effect. As soon as she got to the office on Monday, she picked up the telephone and called *Gambit,* the artsy newspaper.

"I'd like to place a personals ad, please.

"Yes. It should read, 'SWF, attractive redhead twenty-five (about), knows what she wants and ready for fun, loves parties, meeting new people, likes dinner and dancing—seeking good-looking man with dimples (like Mel Gibson?). Don't wait. Call me now.'

"I know it's long," she told the operator, "but I'm in a hurry."

She blushed.

It was exactly seventeen days before Tubby saw Faye Sylvester again. On the Monday morning after the Judge Hughes victory celebration, the first thing Tubby did when he got to his office was fix himself a cup of coffee and chicory and pour in a little cream. Then he got comfortable at the cypress desk that had once belonged to a North Louisiana undertaker. From his perch on the forty-third floor of the Place Palais Building, he could survey the slate roofs of the French Quarter and watch oceangoing vessels power through the hairpin turn of the Mississippi River at Algiers Point. His mind could wander the world.

While it wandered, he opened mail from his clients and gazed at the steamboat *Natchez* working its way lazily toward its berth by the Moon Walk, its decks covered with tiny tourists. He could even hear snatches of the music from the boat's calliope—one of the tricks played by the wind.

Suddenly he exclaimed, "She's coming today!"

Dear Tubby,

I'm coming to the big city next Monday for a conference you might be interested in. I know it isn't considered polite for a lady to ask a man for a date, but I felt we did not really have a chance to talk when you were here. Want to resume?

Call me if you like. I hope you get this letter in time.

From a peaceful place,
Faye

"She's coming today," he said again.
He picked up the phone.

He caught her going out the door.

"Of course it would be great to get together," he assured her. "What's the occasion?"

"Buddy asked me to attend a conference today and tomorrow at Loyola on counseling drug abusers through love. Would you like to join me?"

"Gee, that sounds fascinating," Tubby said, making a face. "Unfortunately, I'm really tied up this afternoon. Would they let you get away for dinner?"

"Sure, I guess so. I'll have to see what the schedule is, but, sure."

"We could do something special. I could cook."

That would be special, she said, and he told her how to find his house.

Flowers reported that afternoon that there was indeed a bug in Judge Hughes's chambers.

He was seated in Tubby's office dressed easy in khaki slacks and a madras shirt. As always, he looked tan and fit. He was also tall, dark, and handsome, and he liked classical music. Tubby knew that because he had ridden in Flowers's car. What the detective did at home was a mystery. Tubby had never been invited for a visit.

"It's not what I'd call a sophisticated device," Flowers explained. "Just a simple audio pickup right under his chair."

"You decommissioned it?"

"The judge told me not to. He said it was in the right place for the message he wanted to deliver."

"Nothing in the phone?"

"There's really no way to tell. The set itself was clean."

"What have you got for me on Marcus Dementhe?"

"It's well known that he's rich and lives off the fortune his father made building subdivisions in Kenner. Harvard undergraduate and a law degree from California Christian. His radio talk show, *Righteous Anger,* led the ratings for three years. His campaign literature said divorced, no children. He grew up in Lakeview. If you remember his ads, he promised to clean up the city. That's a toned-down version of what he used to say on the radio. I tuned him in sometimes when I was working late, and to me he sounded like a Nazi, but that's just a personal opinion. He pays his bills. He was arrested once when he was on spring break from college, but his record was expunged."

"Can't you find any dirt?"

"I'm doing my best, but he seems to be your basic nasty zealot."

"I wonder what caused him to be so aimlessly hurtful?"

"I'm not a shrink. Possibly he wants to be paid to go away."

"You've lived in Louisiana too long."

"I've got to admit I don't understand a man like Dementhe," Flowers said. "There's a million murderers and rapists out there for a district attorney to prosecute. Why doesn't he worry about them?"

"You're not going to charge me for these observations, are you?"

"I wouldn't pay for them, if I were you."

"I guess that's it, then. How's the rest of your business these days?"

"I've got a full plate, but I always give you first priority, you know that. Your jobs are always . . ."

"Always what?"

"Strange?"

"That's me. Anyway, I can't think of anything else for you to do right now."

"Call me if you do," Flowers said.

Raisin and Sapphire were having a late-afternoon Reuben sandwich at Johnny's Po-Boys on St. Ann Street. Raisin was trying not to notice things like the part in her hair, the way her long fingers held the sandwich, and the line of her jaw as she chewed, because he knew from long experience what his fascination with the little things meant. He was getting hooked, and he knew his heart was about to soften up again. It had happened before, with almost all of his women. He had to fight constantly to stay free.

"I guess you're hungry," he said, watching her crunch down a large dill pickle.

"You're a doll to say that," she said, obviously in fantasyland too.

"Mustard on my chin?" she asked.

"No. Is your band playing tonight?"

"I'm off tonight, don't you remember? It's my last Monday off until two weeks from now when the Hot Rocks from Mobile are coming through town."

"Maybe I'll catch your show tomorrow."

"Oh, would you?" she asked happily. "That would be sweet."

"You know, they don't pay you enough for the hours you have to put in."

"At least they pay us something. The dancers actually have to pay the club to work there."

"You're kidding."

"You didn't know that?" She raised a surprised eyebrow. "Mr. Bakustan charges each girl thirty dollars a night to work at the club, and they don't even get free drinks. They're not even supposed to eat anything from the buffet, but if he likes you he doesn't say anything."

"Do you mean all their money comes from tips?"

"You got it. That's why they dream up these scams like the 'Super Orgy' or the 'Cat Walk' so they can make some dough."

"The 'Super Orgy' sounds interesting."

"That's the way it's supposed to sound, but it's a racket. They say to the guy, 'Do you want to come in the back room with me for an orgy?' and he thinks, gee, that will be good. She says, 'It's fifty bucks, pay in advance.' They get the money and take the guys in the back and do some special dances, which are, I am sure, pretty dirty, and they say that's it. That's the orgy. The guy is pissed, but by then they've already got the money."

"Don't they even, you know, give the customer a hand job or something?"

"Not that I know of. You've got to go to the massage parlors for that."

"Or I could take a taxi ride with you."

"In your dreams. Oh, there's Twila." Sapphire

leaned over the table, collecting bread crumbs with her ample bosom, and tapped on the glass. She caught the attention of the freckle-faced loiterer.

Twila brightened in recognition and hurried into the restaurant, pushing through the line of people waiting for takeout.

"I've been looking for you," she told Sapphire breathlessly. "I've got a line on that creep. I met a girl who works for him."

Raisin was not sure which creep she meant. He hid behind his sandwich and took a large bite. It was Italian sausage, dressed with lettuce, tomatoes, and pickles.

"The guy who puts the ads in the paper?"

"Yeah. I asked around like you told me to, and one of the girls at the Tomcat Inn recognized him from the description. She's even been to a party at his house, though it was all straight and aboveboard according to her."

"My name is Raisin," Raisin said.

"I'm sorry. I didn't introduce you. Twila is a friend of mine for as long as I've lived in the Quarter."

"Our cats are best friends," Twila said.

"That's a bond," Raisin agreed.

"Who is the guy?"

"I don't know his name, but this girl Bonnie does. She hangs out with a rave crowd, if you know what I mean. She'll be at their concert tonight. She's one of the drummer's groupies. That's the best place to find her."

"Oh, boy," Sapphire said. "I can't wait to catch that guy Harrell."

"What are you going to do when you find him?" Raisin asked.

"You can punch him out for me."

"If that's what you want, I'm your guy." Raisin might have been serious.

"Or at least tell him we know what he's doing and we're going to turn him over to the cops if he keeps putting those advertisements in the newspapers."

"Punching him out might have a greater effect," Raisin said.

"But I mainly want to see him in the light of day and just walk right up to him and tell him what a true asshole he is. Will you go with me to find Bonnie?" She was addressing Raisin.

"Why not?" Her date checked his watch. "I've got time." It would soon be happy hour. He could handle anything after that.

Tubby's plan to cook a special meal for Faye had boiled itself down to picking up a couple of porterhouse steaks at Langensteins to grill in the backyard. First, he had in mind that they would sit outside and eat some cheese and maybe drink a beer, make that lemonade.

He saw Faye's hippie van when he pulled into his driveway. He had left a key under the mat for her, and she was already inside, poking around in the kitchen.

"You keep a strange pantry," she told him. Tubby dropped his briefcase on a chair.

"You mean empty?"

"I mean five gallons of olive oil, a huge bag of

pistachio nuts, the biggest jar of crushed garlic I've ever seen, five kinds of cheese, and two honeydew melons. That's about it. What do you live on?''

"What you just said. That's what I eat." He was a little embarrassed.

"Do you have a name for this diet?"

"Yeah, 'Garlic-lusters.' Have you ever heard of that?''

"No. Does it involve a beer? Because I'd like one."

Tubby fetched a Coke from his grocery bag and offered it apologetically. She shrugged and accepted it with a smile. He got a ginger ale for himself.

"What time do you have to get back to your meeting?'' he asked.

"There's a film on at eight o'clock that I'm supposed to see.''

"Has the conference been worthwhile so far?"

"I suppose. What they're saying, we already knew. If everybody lived in a place where they were fed and loved, most of the world's problems would disappear.''

"Do you think it's really that simple? Aren't some people just bad?''

"Yes, there are bad people," she said thoughtfully, "but I still believe love can help most of us."

She stood at the back door and looked through the glass at the leaves in the fading sunlight.

"You have a nice yard," she said.

"Thanks. That reminds me. If you've got to get back by eight, I'd better light the coals.''

She put her hand on his chest when he came to the door.

''I hate to tell you this, but I don't eat meat.''

''Are you a vegetarian?'' It was nice to stand this close.

''Sort of,'' she said. ''Would you like to kiss me?''

He smiled, and she smiled back.

11

No one ever saw Purvis, and that was a lucky thing. He lived in the crawl space underneath a shotgun house on Burdette Street. He kept to himself and only slipped out at night to raid the Dumpster at the grocery store a few blocks away. Sometimes days passed when he did not emerge, but through a crack under the front porch, he could watch the comings and goings of people's feet on the sidewalk. Most of the time he just hid.

Purvis sometimes caught a rat, and once he had trapped a cat and eaten it. His drinking supply was a cold-water pipe under the kitchen that dripped into a pet-food can. He could hear the woman's footsteps on the wooden floor above his head. He could also listen in on her conversations, though they didn't make much sense to him.

Once he had lived in the upstairs, as it seemed to him, of this house, but that was a long time ago when he was married. Back before his wife had run him off with her lawyer and a dog. He was, in fact, under the impression that the woman thumping about above him was his wife, not realizing that she had moved to Thibodaux three years before with a man who raised gourds.

The footsteps actually belonged to an old woman who rented the house from a man in Slidell. He kept the rent low because she was on a longshoreman's pension, but mainly because she never complained about anything like the deteriorating neighborhood or the tall weeds in the tiny yard. Or when her cat disappeared.

The little man had only the vaguest sense of the passage of seasons, but this had been an especially thankful Thanksgiving for him. He had found someone who was even less demanding than he was.

First, on a midnight foray for sustenance, from a hiding place under a bush, he saw a car speed away from the grocery-store parking lot. Then, as he hopped from the shadows into the open door of the Dumpster, there she was. Curled up and still, hair pasted over a still-wet spot on her temple.

With great effort Purvis dragged and carried his find to his crawl space, careful to stay out of sight. He set her up on his blanket, on which was written an inscription he had often puzzled over—FT. WALTO ACH. He shared what he had with her. It gave him great satisfaction to comb her hair and dress and undress her.

There came a time, however, when her very presence seemed to became too large and ripe for his space, and he became concerned about the attraction she seemed to exert upon a great many insects and a neighbor's dog. Respectfully, he tugged her out one night and laid her gently in the tall weeds growing around a telephone pole by the street. Once back in the solitude of his den he was glad that she was gone. He heard the bedsprings creak above him and laid his head down to sleep.

12

"This is not my thing. I've got to tell you that up front." Raisin was not pretending to enjoy himself.

"You've got a bad attitude," Sapphire told him.

"I may go berserk and embarrass you in front of your friends."

"Loosen up." She patted his blue-jeaned butt. They were in a long line waiting to get into the rock scene at an old cotton warehouse that had been converted into a rave hall. The gang of teenagers behind them got into a contest to see who would do the most obnoxious thing with a rubber football, and one of them jostled Sapphire from behind.

"Hey, dude," Raisin said, but she stepped on his toe and told him to shut up.

Loud music like elephants mating pounded out of the barn doors, which were guarded by a huge bearded man with a cutoff Harley-Davidson T-shirt. He was sitting on a stool and collecting ten-dollar bills.

"Don't I know you?" Raisin asked, trying to make out the face behind the red sunglasses and tangled yellow beard.

"Da Nang, 1969," the toad said through a hole in the hair.

"I don't think so," Raisin said thoughtfully, but he couldn't finish the reminiscence before he was herded into the dark hall by the crowd behind him.

"I'm in a generation gap," Raisin moaned.

"Hold my hand," Sapphire cried over the music. "The girl we're looking for has a tattoo of a tongue on her forehead."

A band called Galactic Fellatio was banging away at one end of the warehouse. A rotating strobe light on the ceiling, that the producers might have rescued from a wedding-reception ballroom, and a thousand handheld glow sticks provided most of the light. Raisin noticed bundles of electrical cables snaking across the floor. The place looked like maybe yesterday longshoremen with forklifts had cleared out all the cotton. Tonight, juiced-up kids were dancing and falling over each other.

"Where's the bar?" Raisin yelled.

She pointed to the far wall, where there was some encouraging neon.

"I'll meet you back here in ten minutes," he roared. "Want anything?"

She shook her head. Sapphire was busy scanning the room, jumping from toe to toe, trying to spy her friend— the one who knew where the man from the newspaper lived.

Raisin pushed his way across the floor. The people

whose feet he was stepping on were about evenly divided between short-haired types with baseball caps worn backwards and a more diverting breed with spiked hair, acrylic makeup, and ring collections on their noses and lips. Lots of them had plastic bottles hanging from their necks on nylon cords. The girls wore slips longer than their dresses. Quite a few had baby pacifiers stuck in their mouths, wore pants like potato sacks, and were gyrating like Sufis. He saw tattoos galore. There were flowers and birds and gargoyles, penises and ice cream cones, sunsets and ankhs and thunderbolts, but he didn't see any tongues.

He reached the tangle where drinks were being served from ice chests tended by a pair of guys with lots of muscles and gold chains.

"Beer!" he bellowed, when one finally looked his way.

"Coke or spring water," the kid yelled back.

"Ah, shit," Raisin cursed, and barged away.

"Want to buy some vodka?" a pretty girl with a lip bracelet whispered in his ear. Instead of a blouse she wore lace from Yvonne LaFleur's. He nodded and she pulled a clear plastic flask from a fold in her floor-length chemise and showed him five fingers twice.

Why not? He dug a bill out of his wallet, and she traded for the bottle. He took the precaution of unscrewing the cap and sniffing before he let the money go. Sure enough, it had that memorable distilled smell. Lots of other people's money was changing hands around him, he saw. Life Savers, breath mints, and matchboxes all were being passed around for unusually large sums.

Being a streetwise kind of a guy, he suspected these kids were trafficking in the *d*-word. The fact that there were also funny cigarettes burning everywhere tipped him off too.

A pimply-faced girl naked from the waist up gave him a quick hug and moved on, followed by her fans. He could not see Sapphire anywhere.

Hi-ho, he told himself, and tilted his bottle back. Should have got a Coke for a chaser, he thought.

Hi-ho, he said again, as the room morphed into a purple onion. "Should have closed a cockatiel for dinner," he said out loud.

A stampede of bison pounded past, and he wondered why his eyeballs wouldn't stay in his head where they were supposed to be. They were bouncing around all the bare-assed Egyptians eating golden apples in the icebox.

Sapphire pressed her nose to his leer, and before their mind-meld became complete she was replaced by a woman with two mouths and a nipple on her lip. She expressed some concern about his condition. He sensed that he might be a lost little boy and was relieved when a hand took his and induced him to walk.

Enchanted, in slow motion, he considered the infinite variety of humanity as its many forms presented themselves to him. He quickly decided he would greatly prefer solitude in a woodland glen. Tears of gratitude slipped from his eyes when he inhaled some fresh air and saw familiar stars above. They broke apart in a fountain of diamonds. The exhilaration of the thrust when his big engines kicked in caused him to snort like a horse, and he rocketed off into space.

Sapphire got him onto the streetcar, arresting the conductor's alarmed expression with a stony glare, and prayed that Raisin would just shut up.

"The air is full of pixies," he crooned.

Cherrylynn had primped for her date with man number five. She had gotten five responses to her ad in the paper. Part of what she received for $29.95 was a package deal including a voice mailbox where callers could leave messages describing themselves. The one who said he was a Tulane student and the one with the Australian accent she could eliminate. Likewise the guy who said he was from Shreveport and the one who worked seven-on and seven-off on an oil rig. That left a deep voice that said, "My name is Harry. Yes, I like to dance. Give me a call when you're tired of dead ends. Your ad is really cool. You won't be sorry."

Setting aside her first four suitors for a rainy day, she returned "Harry's" call and, of course, got his message service.

Since that first call they had swapped messages several times, and he asked her out. When he suggested meeting at a coffee shop on St. Charles Avenue, she was sure she had her man. They made a date for Wednesday afternoon without ever actually talking in person.

Cherrylynn wore a short gray skirt for the occasion and a black sweater and thought she looked smart. She carried her mocha latte to a table in the corner where she could watch two men in dashikis playing chess.

She became quite engrossed and did not notice the person behind her until a voice said, "Are you Cherrylynn?"

"Oh," she said, looking around. "You're a lot better looking than Mel Gibson."

13

"It's a Mary Kay cosmetics party, dear. I'm afraid I'll be gone all afternoon." Norella Finn was sprucing up her hair with delicate finger flicks. She was short, compact, and dark—a sultry Latin, she called herself. The mirror she was using covered the entire wall of the living room in what the Finns called their boathouse. She could watch the reflection of her husband, who was reading a yachting magazine and sipping a cup of coffee, sitting on one of the straw-and-chrome barstools. Beside him were the spiral stairs that led to the bedroom above, and behind his bowed head was the picture window through which he could keep an eye on his sleek thirty-eight-foot OmniMach HydroRocket, driven by twin 454 V-8 engines. The boat was safely hoisted above the water in its shed.

"You will miss me, won't you?" She kissed him lightly on the cheek.

"Uh-huh," he mumbled, not looking up.

"What are you going to do without me?" she asked.

"Lucky called. He may have a deal I'm interested in. And I've got to be here when the painter comes by to finish up." He used a paper towel to dab up a drop of coffee before it could slip onto his white shorts or matching polo shirt with a red crawfish stitched onto the pocket. "Later tonight I have business downtown."

She left the mirror to poke around in the cushions of the white leather sofa that wrapped around part of the room in search of her purse.

"You are gone too often at night. Last night and the night before you had business. It makes me wonder," she said, almost as an aside.

"That's the name of the game, honey. I don't make the money unless I hang with the high rollers."

Norella came up with a pink leather bag and checked her mirror again.

"I was hoping this evening we could eat at home. Maybe I would give you a back rub in our great big bed."

Their real house was a mile away, but they spent more time out on the lake than they did at home.

"Better if we stay here tonight," Finn said, flipping a page. He did not give any explanation. "Have we got enough beer?"

"I can pick some up if you want. That's what wives are for." She came up behind him and bit him on the ear, careful not to smear her lipstick. "Don't work too hard while I am gone."

"Not likely," he said, and she slipped out the door into the bright sunshine. Seagulls floated hopefully above the boat launch, and Lake Pontchartrain stretched flat as far as the eye could see. She jumped into her red Miata, flipped on the air-conditioning, and was gone.

Jamal, a little stoned, was almost in a trance, pushing his old red lawn mower through the high grass of Mrs. Chin's yard on Burdette Street. The mower's blade was slightly loose, which made it click in jitterbug time and caused the motor to vibrate all the way up to Jamal's back and arms. It was almost soothing him to sleep. Nothing but crumpled beer cans and oyster shells to look out for anyway. Mrs. Chin called him once a month, whenever she got her check, and he tried to keep her yard in tolerable shape. Not much to it, really. Mrs. Chin was half blind anyhow.

He finished mowing her driveway, which had not been used in so long that the gate in the chain link fence along the front of the small yard was rusted shut.

Deliberately, he followed her flower bed as closely as he dared until he got to the broken concrete walkway. He paused to catch his breath, eyeing the stretch between the sidewalk and the curb. The grass and weeds were really overgrown there—about knee high by the telephone pole that marked the corner of her domain. He aimed for the pole on his first pass. The poor engine almost choked in the tall grass, and Jamal woke up a little. Sweating from the exertion, he forced the machine's small wheels closer to the tall mound around the pole. Black smoke belched from the exhaust.

Something shiny caught his attention as he chugged

into the deepest grass. He pulled his overheated machine out of the way and let it idle so he could stoop down and pick up the litter.

He stopped suddenly—stubby fingertips an inch from something glittery. He tried to process what he was seeing. Gold-painted nails on a stiff brown hand.

"Lordy!" he exclaimed, and jumped back. Cautiously, he inched forward again and pushed the weeds away with the tip of his shoe. It was a human hand he saw, and it was connected to an arm. He could make out a faded blue fabric covering a shoulder and, under a nest of twigs, what might be a jaw. He closed his eyes and turned away so he would not have to see any more.

Jamal glanced around wildly, but he did not notice anybody looking at him. Mrs. Chin was back in her house somewhere. The row of shotguns across the street all had their doors closed against the afternoon sunshine. Some kids down on the corner were playing with a jump rope, just like they had probably been doing since they got out of school.

None of my business, Jamal told himself, mad at whoever had left this mess outside where a poor yard-man might stumble on it.

Heart pumping, he revved up his mower and reversed course. Trying to recover his air of detachment, he carved a semicircular edge around the hummock by the pole and, as quickly as he could, finished the rest of the yard. Pausing only to mop off his forehead, he hoisted his old clunker back onto the bed of his pickup truck.

He knocked on Mrs. Chin's door, and as always, it

took her a long time to answer. Propped up by her cane, she pushed open the screen.

"You must be trying to set a record," she told Jamal sternly. "You ain't never finished this quick before."

He dropped his eyes. "Yes, ma'am," he said. "I try to earn my ten dollars."

He had to wait again, shivering in the hot sun, while she tottered back inside to get his pay.

Next door Mr. Armstrong rocked slowly on his porch, concealed from view behind a fig tree. He had watched Jamal hesitate by the hump, and seen him jump back. Mr. Armstrong scratched his white whiskers and shook his head. His eyes had been on that stand of grass for two days now, wondering what he should do. The yardman had not been the first to stick his nose in that spot. Every reaction had been the same. One of the boys from the city garbage truck had stumbled off the curb and endured the jeers of his co-workers, so anxious was he to get away.

"It's a hard world, ain't that the truth," Mr. Armstrong said out loud, but there was nobody around who cared what he had to say.

14

Tubby was at his desk trying to look busy when Cherrylynn asked him on the intercom if he had time to meet with her.

Fearing the worst, that she would tell him she had a new job, he nevertheless invited her to come in.

"I don't want any bad news," he said as she took a chair. She faced him calmly.

"What's that? Oh, no. This has nothing to do with me. I mean it does, but it's different."

"Ah." Tubby sat back, relieved.

"I found the man who suckered Sapphire and paid Sultana to come on to Judge Hughes."

"You what?" he asked incredulously.

"I put a personals ad in the paper," she told him. The guy who calls himself Harry answered my ad, and I met him. I followed him home. I know where he lives. I have his real name—Max Finn—and his phone number."

Satisfaction glowed in her eyes, in part because her employer was at a loss for words.

"What does that mean, you followed him home?" he asked finally.

"Just that. We ate dinner together and then I told him we just didn't click and I would take a cab home. He didn't believe I would dump him, but I did. I told the cabdriver to ride around the block, and we saw him get his car from the valet. We followed him home."

"Very interesting. How did you get his name and phone number?"

"From the city directory at the library this morning. With a street address you can find out anything."

"That's quite impressive, my dear. What possessed you to do all of this without telling me?"

"I wanted to."

"I see. Well, I think I would like to talk to this man without further delay. Can I have the number?"

Cherrylynn pushed a piece of paper across the desk. Tubby looked at it and picked up his telephone.

"What did you order for dinner?" he asked while it rang.

"It was called Trout Smilie. They roll a trout fillet in bread crumbs and top it with crabmeat. It's baked in wine."

"That's the name of the restaurant? Smilie's?" The phone was still ringing.

"Right."

* * *

An arrow of sunlight crossed the carpet where Finn lay on his face. It disappeared when the door softly closed. On the wall the telephone began to ring. Eventually, it stopped.

"Nobody there," Tubby said as he placed the receiver back on the hook. "I've never been to Smilie's. Perhaps we could go together." He stared out the window at a bank of clouds rolling in from the west. "Maybe I should drive out to the lake right now and see if I can find this Max Finn guy."

"I'd like to go with you," Cherrylynn said.

"I guess if you 'want to,' that's what you're going to do."

"Right," she said again. "You owe me twenty-eight dollars for the taxicab."

"Write yourself a check out of the office account." Tubby collected his things. "If you 'want to,' of course. By the way. Did you find this guy was the irresistible lover everybody says he is?"

"Not my type," she said. "I don't go for the wavy hair." Tubby quickly passed his hand over his own fore-head, trying to flatten out any curls.

Nikki mopped the perspiration off the back of his neck and stuck a folded blue tarp under his arm. He locked the white truck with NIKKI'S PAINTING stenciled on it and walked slowly to the red door of the boathouse.

He knocked and waited patiently. Droplets trickled under his collar. He knocked again and groaned.

"Ms. Finn. Oh, Mr. Finn. Nikki's here. The painter."

He rocked from foot to foot. He had called ahead, only three hours ago. Mr. Finn had told him to come on.

"Hello?" He rapped on the door, and it pushed open.

"Well." Nikki put his foot inside on the carpet. A burst of cool air invited him to advance. "Painter here. . . ."

The feet on the floor, shod in white Docksides, weren't moving. Nikki took another step and saw the top of Mr. Finn's head behind the sofa. The face was plum colored and locked in a grimace so tight, the teeth were bared. Finn's eyes bulged out and stared lifelessly at the intruder.

Nikki screamed and covered his face with his hands. He stumbled all the way out of the door, back in the blazing sun, before he dared to look again.

Tubby piloted his baby-blue Chrysler out the interstate, where the rush-hour traffic was finally subsiding. The evening was turning cloudy as some distant storm started to blow in. When they got off at West End Boulevard, gusts of hot wind were kicking around the tall trees lining the street.

"Doesn't look like we'll see much of a sunset," he said.

"I like the water in a storm," Cherrylynn replied. "I've always thought it looks exciting."

"Sometimes too exciting. Don't forget Hurricane Georges. That sucker missed us by a hundred miles and still made the Mississippi River run backwards."

"It's our own fault if we haven't got any better sense than to live near the Gulf of Mexico."

They turned at the marina, passed the restaurants that had been rebuilt after the last storm, and then a choppy inland sea was before them.

"I think the address is right up ahead," Tubby said, rounding a bend.

"Whoa," Cherrylynn exclaimed. He stepped hard on the brakes.

The street was blocked by police cars, lights flashing, and an ambulance was backed up to the curb.

Tubby followed the officer's wave and detoured into the parking lot of the public boat launch. Other cars were making a U-turn and leaving the area, but Tubby found a parking space and, with Cherrylynn trotting behind, hurried up to the police line to see what was going on.

There were quite a few spectators, and one of them turned around and gave a mocking salute.

"How's it going, boss?" Raisin Partlow asked. "Did y'all come to gawk at the dead body? You remember Sapphire, don't you?"

He did, from the videotape.

"They're bringing him out now," Sapphire announced dreamily.

Without asking for an explanation of this coincidental meeting, Tubby and Cherrylynn pushed up to the yellow tape and watched two women in white coats wheel a sheet-covered gurney out of the front door of a chartreuse boathouse with a red door. They bounced it over the sidewalk and, with a sudden shove, sent the cadaver sliding into the back of the wagon.

"Do you know who it is?" Tubby asked. He observed that Cherrylynn was intent on the ambulance attendants.

"Cop said it was the man of the house, and the neighbor said the man was Max Finn."

"That's the guy we came to see."

"Same with us. Looks like we got here too late."

"What happened to him?"

"I don't know. The police aren't saying. We're here because Finn was the man who trapped Sapphire with that phony personals ad. I thought you weren't interested in that case."

"This Finn also seems to be connected to something else I'm working on," Tubby explained vaguely.

"I guess that's a bad coincidence, since he's dead."

There was a commotion behind them. The sightseers' heads turned to watch a short black-haired woman running through the parking lot. She passed within a few feet of Raisin, and a policeman tried to stop her from ducking under the tape.

"Is it my husband?" she screamed. "You get the hell out of my way! Is it my husband?" She lifted the tape over her head and made a beeline for the gaping back door of the ambulance. Tubby immediately recognized the woman.

"Norella!" he yelled. "Officer, I'm that woman's lawyer."

"Keep back, buddy, unless you want to spend the night in jail." The policeman sounded bored.

The woman turned briefly when she heard her name. She seemed to see Tubby, but her eyes weren't focused. She remembered her purpose and tried to jump inside the ambulance. One of the EMTs pushed her back, and a detective in street clothes grabbed her arm and pulled her firmly though the red door of the boathouse.

"I'm that woman's lawyer. I want to see her," Tubby insisted.

"Listen, dude," the cop said, "this here's a crime scene, and it has to stay clear."

Norella was not actually Tubby's client, but he knew her. Not very long ago she had been the romantic interest of his friend Jason Boaz, the inventor. Still, Tubby could not stand by while she was manhandled by the NOPD.

He ducked under the ribbon and scurried past the surprised policeman. Since he had a good head start, he made it to the sidewalk before the bellowing cop caught up with him.

While the officer roared and reached for his cuffs, and the crowd cheered Tubby on, a plainclothesman rushed outside to see what was the matter.

"Stand back, I'm a lawyer!" Tubby cried.

"Oh, Tubby, please help me," Norella screamed from the room inside.

"Who the hell are you?" the detective in charge wanted to know.

They managed to get it sorted out without anyone getting arrested.

The deceased was indeed Max Finn.

The detective was LeBoeuf Kronke. On closer inspection he remembered Tubby, having once interrogated him regarding the murder of a dockworker named Broussard.

Norella Finn, formerly Norella Peruna of Honduras, was the widow.

By virtue of butting in Tubby was now her lawyer.

She was not, however, under arrest or even under suspicion at the moment, and the detective had only pulled her out of the ambulance to determine her identity, he said. Unfortunately, she was not free to go just yet because the detective wanted to talk to her. And she did not want to go because, in the midst of this tragedy, she had nowhere else to be.

Tubby could either stick around or split, it was up to him. Just stay out of the medical examiner's way and don't touch anything, he was told.

"Well, actually I have some friends outside," Tubby hedged.

"Oh, Tubby, don't leave me," Norella sobbed.

He was stuck, but fortunately detective Kronke ushered in the next-door neighbor, a large effusive woman who immediately embraced Tubby's delirious client and began consoling her with peeps and coos like a giant pigeon courting.

Not bothering to ask for anyone's permission, the neighbor stood Norella up and marched her out of the gloomy house. They went next door.

Left with nothing to do, Tubby wandered. He halted spellbound when he beheld the speedboat suspended outside the picture window at the rear of the house.

"What kind of a boat is that?" he asked the patrolman taking pictures of the chalk outline of nobody on the plush cream carpet.

Tubby had never been in such a boat. His experience was with the kind of vessel that rode a trailer, pulled water skis, and had a built-in well for storing bait. "Damn thing must top sixty miles an hour," he said to himself.

"Lieutenant said it would go one hundred and eighty," the cop whispered.

"I'll be damned," Tubby said. The craft reminded him that there was a public boat launch outside and that he had deserted his friends in the parking lot.

"Guess I'll be going," he told anyone who cared to listen, and scampered out the door.

The ambulance was still there, and some of the crowd, and so was the sizable cop who had tried to bust him.

Tubby stayed well away from that gentleman when he bent under the tape and tried to melt back into the ring of spectators.

He found Cherrylynn leaning against his car. She was smoking a cigarette but stepped on it when Tubby walked up.

"What happened to Raisin?" Tubby asked.

"He and his girl left. She said as long as Finn was dead she didn't need to stick around. You and Mr. Raisin aren't friends anymore?"

"Sure. Why do you ask that?"

She looked away, toward the lake and the waves rolling in. "You ought to make peace with him," she said.

"Thanks for the advice. You want to get something to eat?"

"I'd rather go home and take a bath," she said. "Death is dirty."

15

At his office Tubby was waiting for Norella Peruna Finn to show up.

Cherrylynn stuck her head in the door.

"Mr. Boaz called," she reported. The sullenness of recent days was still in her voice.

"Thank you so much. That's a very nice dress you're wearing." He was trying to induce an improved mood.

"Gracias," she said, giving him a half smile, "I've had it for years."

"Oh."

She turned and pranced out.

"My mistake," he said to her back.

He wondered if Cherrylynn had a real boyfriend these days. It had been a while since she had mentioned one. Problems in the romance department might explain her testiness and her tardiness.

He cast aside thoughts of Cherrylynn's sex life, picked up the phone, and punched in Jason's number.

"Speak," the voice at the other end of the line commanded.

"Good morning, Jason, this is Tubby."

"My man, I've got a new idea I want to run by you." Jason was always full of new ideas. Many were flaky, but the good ones had made him big money. It was how he made his living. He paid Tubby to protect his strange notions with patents.

"I'm all ears."

"It involves men's ties. They're a drag to wear, as I'm sure you know, and they cost fifty bucks apiece. We can avoid all that by painting a picture of a tie directly on the shirt."

This was not going to be one of the good ones, Tubby feared. Jason supplied a few more details. There might be some potential here. Hell, Tubby knew he was no judge of what would sell and what wouldn't.

"What say we meet at the Fairgrounds and watch the ponies race a few. You can run your meter."

"I'm real busy these days, Jason. Couldn't we get together at my office?"

"Say again?"

"Let's meet here."

"Tubby, that's the first time I heard you say no to the Track."

"Well, you know, you've got to buckle down and work sometimes."

"That's middle-aged thinking, my boy."

"Sure, but we're middle aged. I saw your old girl-friend yesterday."

"Which one?" Jason was suspicious.

"Norella."

"Yeah? Must have been with her new husband. He's into boats and money and all that stuff."

"Her ex-husband, Max Finn. He died." It crossed Tubby's mind that Jason might somehow be involved in this mess, but he dismissed the thought as absurd.

"Sweet Mary, that's a shame. Did she kill him?"

"I don't think so. Why would you say that?"

"She's high-strung and flighty, and mean in short spurts."

"No, I don't think she killed him. It's not even clear yet what he died from."

"She'll have a new man soon."

"You think?"

"Norella is a special, beautiful butterfly. She flits from flower to flower. I haven't see her since she threw a Scotch and soda in my lap at the Red Saloon. I might not see her for another year, but when I do she'll give me a wicked smile and a kiss. She'll say she's been thinking about me all the time."

"Jason, nobody could forget you."

"That's true, I guess. How about tomorrow at one. As a compromise, let's eat at the Redfish Grill."

Tubby said that would be just fine.

Norella was sobbing on the sofa. Tubby was behind his desk, suffering.

"Did the police find any sign of forced entry?" He was looking at his yellow pad.

"No." There was a vacant look in her red-rimmed eyes. Her hair was askew. Her hands were clasped between her brown knees.

"Have you noticed anything missing?"

She shook her head.

"What did your husband do with that boat?" he asked. The attractive image of the sleek spear-shaped hull appeared in his mind.

"He liked to race," she said simply. "But it is a very expensive thing to have, such a boat."

"Exactly what kind of work was your husband in, Norella?" He watched her out of the corner of his eye. She seemed to hesitate.

"Finn had lots of money in the stock market. And he gambled. He made big deals with lots of important people."

"What about his escort service?"

"What escort service?"

"Well, let's start with a woman named Sapphire Serena and another woman named Sultana Patel. He paid them to go to parties. Ring any bells?"

"That's bullshit!" she said indignantly. "I never heard anything about that."

"Really? Well, did you ever see him with strange women?"

"Of course not. How foolish." Norella blew her nose loudly in her hankie.

"That's what you told the police?"

"Sure." She looked up at him, all innocence.

His eyebrows did push-ups. "Maybe that's why they consider you a suspect," he said.

"That is insane. I am his wife. I had nothing to do with this."

"Who do you think did?"

"He's had arguments with Lucky LaFrene. They had some kind of business deal that went bad."

"Lucky LaFrene the car dealer?"

"That's him."

"You think Lucky LaFrene might have killed your husband? He's a millionaire."

"What difference does that make?" Her Latin eyes flashed.

"Norella, just what is it you want me to do?" he asked in exasperation.

"Get me out of this," she hissed, "Poor Max is not the point. I just don't like death. Max had money. I want my share. I don't want this." Her arm swept around the office, taking in her life. "I'll sell the boathouse. I'll sell our home. I just want to get out."

Dodging potholes in the dark, the nondescript Chevy Blazer raced down Magazine Street—a blue light spinning on its dashboard. Daneel had a death grip on the steering wheel, and Johnny Vodka was fumbling with his pistol, making sure the clip was full. When they passed Napoleon Avenue, Vodka flipped off the flashing light.

"That could be him," he said, urgently pointing across the street to a tall figure in a dark overcoat hurrying toward them.

"We'll find out!" Daneel hit the brakes and careened over the curb, sliding to a stop an inch from a no-parking sign. The suspect abruptly ducked onto a side street and vanished in the shadows. With the motor still knocking the policemen piled out, guns in hand, and sprinted after him.

In his haste Vodka slipped on a pop bottle and twisted his ankle.

"You okay?" Daneel called over his shoulder.

"Yeah," Vodka grunted, limping as fast as he could. "Where did he go?"

Cars were parked on both sides of the narrow street. The neighborhood was a mixture of shotgun houses and bricked-up commercial establishments crowded together.

"In there, I think." Daneel gestured with his pistol at a gray cinder-block building set back from the street. A rusty sign said SHEET METAL WORKS.

Warily Daneel approached a steel door and tried the handle. The door creaked open.

Vodka nodded at him.

Daneel slid inside and his partner followed, trying to be thin.

The interior was black as ink and smelled of grease and chemicals. A noise ahead of them like a file scraping across a pipe caused both cops to crouch and point their weapons.

Somewhere glass broke.

"Police!" Vodka yelled. "Show yourself and nobody gets hurt!"

"Can't see a goddamn thing," Daneel muttered,

groping along the wall for a light switch. He found a lever and pulled it.

Expecting illumination he was instead enveloped by the deafening roar of gears grinding into action and a frightening flapping overhead as though some huge bird's sleep had been disturbed.

In his surprise Vodka jumped on his gimpy ankle, which gave way, and he crumpled onto the floor, cursing. He nearly discharged his gun into his leg.

Daneel spun around, searching for the source of the noise. Frantically he banged along the wall, punching buttons and flipping switches. Suddenly the ceiling lights came on, revealing a vast network of machines and pulleys. The flapping noise above came from a belt that ran the length of the room, powering the mysterious system.

Vodka sat cross-legged on the cement.

"Police," he said weakly. "Give it up."

Not far away a black sedan started up and drove slowly into the night, its headlights off.

Inside the factory the policemen got the presses turned off. They searched the interior until broken glass and an open door at the back convinced them that they had lost their quarry.

It was a bitter disappointment. A fifteen-year-old girl, dropped off after a party, had been assaulted two blocks away. Somewhere in the city was a brutal man who liked to hate young women. Vodka and Daneel had been after him for three months. Lately he seemed hungrier.

16

The black mongrel that hung out by the pool hall lifted his leg to pee on the telephone pole. Enraptured by a new scent, he sniffed at the edge of the tall weeds. He recognized the body as being human, but never had he encountered a lifeless one thrown out with the trash.

He grabbed the arm with his teeth and shook it, determined to get a response.

Disappointed, he growled and fought tenaciously, tugging at his discovery with such intensity that most of the body came flopping out into the street. Ants had been at work. They boiled out at the distraction.

Uncertain what to do, the dog started running in circles around the body. A car driving down the street had to slow down or hit the dog. The driver stuck his head out of his window, blew his horn to scare the mutt, and quickly accelerated away.

The big woman who lived across the street came out on her porch to tell the dog to shut up, but she got curious enough to go down her steps to investigate. She saw the head of hair and the gold fingernails and figured out the rest.

"Oh, Jesus," she screamed at the top of her lungs. "Somebody call nine one one."

Cherrylynn was taking a long lunch—maybe having a job interview somewhere, Tubby feared—so he was working the phones himself.

He kept trying, off and on, to reach Sultana Patel, the key witness against Al Hughes and now the key to his entrapment defense, but her phone just rang and rang.

He called his client, the judge, but Hughes's secretary, Mrs. Evans, said he absolutely could not be disturbed.

It gave Tubby time to wallow in his own lassitude.

Raisin Partlow, the friend upon whom he had long depended for refreshingly bitter common sense, was in a fool's pursuit of the fountain of youth. Tubby had little desire even to see Raisin these days.

His professional role model, the judge, was in the mud.

His daughters all had lives of their own, and it was frightening how little he knew about them.

And his potential girlfriend, Faye Sylvester? She was trying to lure him to a place far away. But could he breathe there?

All of the familiar landmarks of the town he loved best were disappearing, it was true. The courthouse was in the grip of a district attorney bent on stomping out all the fun in life. Mudbugs dance hall was gone. The Galleria had changed its name. The price of crawfish was up. He was having trouble remembering why it was he loved New Orleans.

He had not tasted alcohol in weeks, and he missed it. Just like he did every day.

The lawyer's dark thoughts were interrupted by a call from his real estate agent.

"Have I found you the perfect spot," she said excitedly. "A two-bedroom house on three acres of land right in Old Mandeville. Cypress trees, Spanish moss, bike path to the lake, the whole bit. It's a steal at two hundred forty thousand dollars. I drove past your house yesterday, and I think you could get almost that much for it if you sold it today. It will be close, of course, but you can't expect to make money when you buy a new house. I could show it to you this afternoon."

"Today? That's pretty soon."

"It won't wait around forever, Tubby. The place is a bargain, and they know it. If you're interested we have to move fast."

"Sure I'm interested. I'm just really busy right now. I didn't expect you to find a place so soon. Maybe next week."

"It may be gone by then."

"Look, I'll call you in a day or two and we'll try to work something out."

"Okay," the realtor said sadly.

Tubby felt guilty for disappointing her. Life was so complicated, all of a sudden.

* * *

It was close to lunchtime when Jason Boaz arrived. He was a burly man with a rich black beard and on this occasion he was sporting a tan fedora. Characteristically exuberant, he created a small commotion upon arriving by giving Cherrylynn a box of chocolates.

"Filled with rum punch," he explained. "Hurricanes, I call them. Experimental, of course. See if you like them."

As they walked out of the office he told Tubby, "That girl is something special, you know. Great telephone personality, a zest for life. You're lucky to have her."

"Yeah, I know," Tubby grumped.

There is something about crossing Canal Street into the French Quarter that makes the world tilt about fifteen degrees. Drudgery and focus are both difficult when you must step around a man sitting on a milk carton playing blues on a sax, when well-dressed German tourists force you off the sidewalk, when children tap-dancing beg you for coins, and when your banker, tie askew, collides with a gas lamp in front of you.

"Great aroma!" Jason exulted, sucking a breeze full of café-au-lait loudly though his nostrils.

"Lots of trash," Tubby replied, kicking a crumpled cup into the gutter.

"You're in a strange mood, my friend. Had your fill of local funk?"

Instead of answering, Tubby cocked his head at a fat lady passed out like a puddle on the steps of a shuttered house. Her stockings were rolled around her ankles and she was mumbling incoherently in her sleep.

"You don't see the charm?" Jason pressed. "Where else in America is a siesta permitted in the doorway of a million-dollar home?"

"Lucky Dog?" a cross-eyed vendor screamed in Tubby's ear.

"Jesus!" he exclaimed, sidestepping the sausage-shaped wagon and shrugging the man off. "I thought he knew my name."

"Lucky as a blind dog in a meat house," Jason said. "Old Cuban proverb."

He stood back to let Tubby precede him into the restaurant.

It was crowded.

"Shall we eat at the bar?" Jason suggested, and Tubby nodded.

It was in fact an oyster bar, and despite his reservations Tubby was inspired to enjoy himself.

"Want to split a dozen?" he asked.

"Let's each get one." Jason raised his long arm like a mast and waved two fingers at the aproned shucker who was industriously prying open the barnacle-studded rocks with his thick knife.

"What else have we got here?" Jason studied the chalkboard above their heads.

"Have you ever had the sweet potato catfish?" he asked.

Tubby had not. Nor had he ever tasted an andouille meat pie, so they placed their orders.

When the waitress departed he invited Jason to lay out his plan.

"Virtual Ties? They're great. I'm wearing one now." Jason displayed his chest. From the collar of his blue shirt hung a red tie full of tiny smiling whales. On closer inspection it was revealed that the tie was actually printed onto the shirt fabric.

"That's pretty neat," Tubby admitted.

"No foolin'," Jason agreed. "We can sell these. I've got some sample drawings. The whole thing is set out in this précis." He tossed a manila envelope at Tubby. "Do what you can with it."

"Don't they already have something like that?" Tubby asked.

"They have something like everything, Tubby, but I'm the first guy you heard it from, right? Anyway, I've got another idea cooking now."

"Okay, shoot."

"You are aware we are in the midst of a cigar craze. Everybody wants to smoke cigars. They're paying ten or twenty bucks apiece for the things."

"Right."

"So I've got a plan for a special cigar that will really capture the public's imagination."

Tubby made encouraging hums.

"We lace these little suckers with crack."

"What?"

"Just checking to see if you were listening. Now, my real idea is completely legal. You've got to realize that half the people who smoke cigars actually can't stand them. They don't like the taste or the smell. It makes them sick, but they have to hide that from their friends.''

"Maybe," Tubby said. Personally, he enjoyed a good cigar, but he had suspected that not everyone around him did.

"Allow me to present to you a 'Cuba Libre' or 'Cigar-Lite' as I call them." He pulled a stogie from his jacket pocket and handed it over lovingly.

"Looks like a cigar, right?"

Tubby agreed that it did. He ran it under his nose.

"Smells like a cigar?"

"It does."

"Well, my friend, that little status symbol is packed with a special blend of lettuce, sugar cane bagasse, and soybean husks, and it burns so light, it merely scents the tongue. Anybody can smoke one. On top of that it puts out a cloud of odorless blue smoke so you can puff it like a locomotive and everybody thinks you're enjoying a real Havana, but you don't get sick. And we can make a companion product with honest-to-goodness real mint leaves ground up in there that makes the Lite as sweet as a Virginia Slim."

"This will sell?"

"God, yes. I can make these babies for ten cents apiece and wholesale them for four dollars. That's what my buddies in the business tell me. And I don't have to go to Cuba for them because there's a guy in Chalmette who can turn them out in his garage."

Jason assumed a serious expression as a patriotic aura settled over him.

"You know, that's what I love about New Orleans,"

he continued, resuming his assault on Tubby's strange mood. "There are people here from all over the world, and they brought their special talents with them. And most of 'em have a sense of humor too. Don't you think? Like this guy. He came here on a wooden boat from Haiti or someplace and he pumps gas in a grease pit out on Judge Perez Highway. But in his garage he has built a cigar-rolling machine, and in his backyard he grows tobacco. And he tells me, 'Mr. Boaz, St. Bernard Parish is de land of golden opportunity.' "

"We have a rich culture," Tubby acknowledged.

"Yeah? You bet we do."

"Sometimes one longs for simplicity, don't you think?"

"Balls!" Jason protested.

"Whatever. As for your cigar, though, I'm not certain this is something you can patent."

"Well, do some research on it. As soon as I line up a guy who can make me a decent box, you know, with gold embossing and cool stuff like that, I'm going into production."

"Who would distribute them?"

"Not known yet. Hell, I'll sell them out of the back of my Mercedes if I have to, just to get started. This is my best idea since the Port-a-Soak."

"What about your state taxes and Uncle Sam?"

"There's not a shred of tobacco in this cigar. The feds don't tax lettuce."

"Maybe I should research that too."

"Please do, but be quick. Surf's up, and I want to ride the wave."

"By the way, Jason, did you ever happen to meet Norella's husband, Max Finn?"

"I've never been invited behind the red door, I'm afraid."

"How did you know their house had a red door?"

Jason rubbed his mustache. "Somebody must have pointed it out to me," he said absently. "Eat your damn oysters. Want some horseradish? Would you like to hear about my hat?"

17

Lucky LaFrene's Chevrolet, Hyundai, Nissan, and Isuzu occupied twenty acres of reclaimed swampland on Veterans Highway. The path inside led past a thousand cars in a dazzling array of colors, almost blinding in the sunshine, and a skirmish line of salesmen in sport coats determined to intercept anyone who tried to slip through with his wallet.

"Ninety days, same as cash," cried one linesman who tried to block Tubby's way. Nimbly the visitor sidestepped.

"Push, tow, or crawl, we trade them all," another one loudly promised.

"You're demented," Tubby muttered.

As he muscled his way through the glass doors into the frigid showroom, his attitude was instantly altered by the vision of the car of his dreams. It was a gleaming red Velocitar, like nothing he had ever seen. Lithe and muscular, lavished with chrome, it spoke to his inner Iron

John. Drive me on the levee, let me wrap my seats of black leather around you, it whispered caressingly.

"She's a beauty, huh?" a man with the wrong coat but gleaming teeth whispered in Tubby's ear.

"Ah," Tubby exhaled. "What's the sticker on that thing?"

"If you have to ask, you probably don't want to know." With this wisdom imparted the man tapped a pencil on his temple.

Tubby leaned forward to look, and his bubble popped. Almost as much as my house, he thought.

"Not bad," he said loudly. "Say, can you tell me where I can find Lucky LaFrene?"

"The boss of bosses? His office is in the back. Maybe I can tell him who's calling."

"Sure. Tubby Dubonnet, from the Al Hughes campaign."

The salesman wobbled away, and Tubby lost himself again in the rich ruby luster of the Velocitar. Why, this baby had a full wet bar in the back and a TV set on the dash. If only the kids would drop out of school, he might have some money. If only the Kleeb settlement would ever come through. If only an injured seaman would hobble into his office. He again pondered the nagging question central to his profession. Should he advertise in the Yellow Pages? The boys who could buy this car probably did.

"Howya doin', Tubby, Tubby, Tubby?" Lucky LaFrene spouted, waddling across the floor.

He pumped Tubby's hand with both of his own.

"Are you car-shopping or just name-dropping?

What's the lowdown, dude? We can deal if you're for real.''

"We met at the Hughes fund-raiser, remember, Lucky?" Tubby worked his hand loose.

"I've gotta memory like a bat trap, bubba. I know you like a glove."

"That's great. Is there someplace we can talk for a minute? I've got something kind of private to discuss with you."

"Confidential, huh?" LaFrene winked and motioned Tubby to follow him. "Let's retire to my inner sanctotum."

LaFrene's office boasted a cluttered desk, a cabinet full of model ships, and a bright orange sofa. The turquoise walls were covered with plaques and awards for automotive one-upmanship and civic loveliness.

"Make yourself comfy," the host invited. "What can I do for a legal beagle?" He settled behind his desk and tossed an executive tension-reducing beanbag into the air. He snatched it with one hand and grinned.

"You know Max Finn?" Tubby asked, keeping an eye on the orbiting sack. "He died day before yesterday."

"Yeah. Sad thing." LaFrene frowned obligingly. "We was campadres from way back. We all called Max 'Twenty-One Gun Salute' at St. Anthony's. Bet you can guess why. We had some times together." A tear oozed out of the corner of his eye. He sniffled.

"I represent his widow, Norella."

"What a lady. She must be totally begrieved. They

was together such a short time. What happened to poor Max? Nobody's sayin' nuthin'.''

Tubby shrugged. ''I was hoping that you might have some idea. Norella leaves the house at noon and everything's fine. By four o'clock he's dead on the floor. She says the last thing he told her was that you were coming to meet him.''

''Me?'' LaFrene let the beanbag plop onto his desk. ''That's a pile of poop-poop-pee-doo. I was nowhere around Max day before yesterday. That's really what she told you?''

''She says that's what Max told her.''

''Must be some kind of misunderstanding. Max and me hung out a lot together, but not when he died, I can promise you that. No, no, not us.''

''What did you do when you hung out?''

''Oh, we was just pals, you know. We'd hoist a few or go out on the boats. Max, you know, was a great sailor. He was planning to sell me his OmniMach HydroRocket. It's really mine. I guess Norella told you that.''

''She didn't mention it.''

This information troubled LaFrene. ''I hope she ain't having any mental magnesia. We already shook hands.''

''I'll ask her. What can you tell me about Max's business?''

''Me? Not much. No, no, can't say what he did. He was a whiz at craps, I'll say that much. He made some dough working the telephones, too, if you call that working. What do I know about it? I'm just a car magnate.''

LaFrene held open his hands to illustrate his humble empire.

"Did you ever know about him being involved with call girls?"

"What the hell's that?"

"You know. Setting up girls with men for parties. Escorts. Hookers, maybe."

"Whoo, he had some fillies, sure, but I don't believe everything I see."

"What's that mean, Lucky?"

"For instance, I once saw a flying saucer right over Lakeside Shopping Center, plain as rain. And I saw it zoom right down Veterans Boulevard all the way to where Clearview is today. In my hot-rod Chevy!" He pounded his desk. "It was just swamp back then. And I wasn't the only one who saw it. But I don't believe it."

LaFrene's benign grin wrestled with Tubby's incredulous stare.

"So," the lawyer resumed, "you saw Finn with different women?"

"I seen him with lots of pretty dames, that's true."

"Did Norella know about it?"

"You just asked me a question I can't answer," LaFrene said primly.

"Let's try this one, then. Who had a reason to kill Finn?"

"So, it was murder. I thought it might be. And, you know, there ain't a single soul I can think of who would permeate such a crime."

"The man had no enemies?"

"He was clean as a golden fleece."

"You gave a party for Al Hughes during the election campaign?"

The change of subject caught LaFrene by surprise, and his eyes narrowed for an instant.

"I was happy to do so. Al's my judge. I've always voted for Al. He's right as a rock."

"There was a young lady who came to that party. Her name was Sultana Patel. Do you know her?"

LaFrene scratched behind his ear.

"Can't say as I do."

"Short, dark, maybe twenty-five, nice looking."

"That don't ring a chord."

"Then I guess you wouldn't know who she came with."

"How could I, Tubby? I don't know who the hell you're talking about."

The lawyer could think of more things to ask, but he couldn't see that he was getting anywhere. Either LaFrene was a fool or he could sure pretend to be one. It was probably the latter, considering all of the diamonds flashing on the car man's fingers. But no matter how you translated LaFrene's remarks, they were not much help. He stood up.

"Thanks for your time, Lucky. If you think of anything that might help Norella make sense out of this tragedy, please give me a call."

"I sure will." LaFrene swept across the room, blowing Tubby out with him. "And don't you forget who gets that boat. We rolled the dice, and I need my slice." He guided Tubby across the showroom, slapped him hard on the back, and pushed him out the door.

Tubby looked back through the glass at the beautiful Velocitar, and there was Lucky LaFrene talking on a portable phone.

18

Todd Murphy was no genius. That's why the LSU medical student was doing his residency in the morgue. No high-price surgeries here. No smooth bedside manner was required.

He made his incision with a practiced hand. There was something in that belly that shouldn't be there. His fingers had detected it. An X ray had confirmed it.

There was no blood. The man had been converted into a body more than sixteen hours ago. That was an educated guess, at least.

Neatly and precisely the assistant coroner pulled apart the dermas and parted the muscles. Ah, there was the stomach, all gray and oysterlike. He prodded and squeezed the heavy organ with his latex-gloved hand, just out of curiosity.

Murphy took a deep breath and held it, anticipating

the burst of gas he was about to release. Then he drew his scalpel through the unresisting tissue.

Right away he saw something foreign. Setting aside his scalpel, Murphy gently extracted a handful of plastic golden disks, like a small treasure from the sea, from the cadaver's gut. On each was engraved, "$1,000 Grand Mal Casino."

"Ah," he said again, with satisfaction.

After some more digging he found another chip stuck in Mr. Finn's windpipe.

Murphy rolled the cadaver away and secured the fifteen golden chips in a clear plastic bag. He held the bag up in front of the light and thought things over.

Then he moved on to his next interesting problem, the unclaimed body in the next drawer. It was time to look at it again. It was also a peculiar case. Some evidence of trauma to the vagina and rectum. Still, that was not what had killed the young female. She appeared to have been malnourished. And she had been sliced across the neck with something sharp. But there were no obvious signs of a struggle.

He had been able to postpone admitting the difficulty of classifying this death because, conveniently, no one had shown up to claim or identify the body. So long had it been left exposed to the elements after death—at least three days, Murphy thought—that most of its features had been eaten away by bugs or rodents, further complicating identification. What was also curious was that one foot had been almost totally hacked off by a crude blade, much like a propeller, and the woman's underwear was on backwards. Once or twice a day, Murphy would pull out the drawer and study the corpse for minutes at a time, searching for clues.

19

Al Hughes chose to meet in the open air. Seems he was paranoid now about eager ears in the walls, not just in his courtroom but in his house, in Tubby's office, and everywhere else. Walking around on the street downtown wouldn't do, because there might be surveillance cameras and long-range listening devices hidden in the highrise buildings. He was worried about restaurants, too, because somebody might overhear his conversations.

"Well, where can we talk?" Tubby was exasperated.

"How about at the zoo," Hughes suggested, so finally the two men were sitting on a wooden bench watching zebras, giraffes, and gazelles graze on a recreated African veldt. School kids and ladies with prams flitted around them. Al had on his idea of a disguise, which was sunglasses and a red tam-o'-shanter. They made him look like a school principal moonlighting as a cabdriver.

Unwilling to starve, Tubby had picked them up a couple of soft-shell crab po' boys at Domilese's.

"Feel safe enough?" he asked when he sat down beside Al and opened his brown paper sack. He was being sarcastic.

"Don't make fun of me, pal. It's not your butt they're after."

"I'm not so sure," Tubby said, thinking about the DA's almost casual comments about his daughter's sex life.

The judge accepted his long sandwich wrapped in white butcher paper. He carefully unfolded his lunch and lifted the bread on top to see what it was loaded with. "Did you put some hot sauce on this?" he asked.

"Yeah. I thought you liked it that way."

Hughes nodded and took a bite. He had to use both hands to hold it together.

"How did your meeting with our friend go?" he asked, mouth full.

"Strangely. The DA seems to feel that you are guilty as charged, and I get the feeling that he has no qualms about destroying your reputation and career if you do not cooperate with his investigation."

The judge shifted uncomfortably on the park bench.

"Great news," he said. "How am I supposed to cooperate?"

"That's the strange part. He didn't reveal any specific target for his snooping, so I guess you can pick and choose which judges on the court you want to incriminate. I get the feeling he thinks all of them are equally corrupt but can't put his finger on anything specific that anybody has actually done."

"Except for me."

Tubby nodded.

"And the sad truth is, most of my colleagues are so honest, they're boring as Mondays. I mean, they all might do a favor for a friend now and then, but nothing important, if you get me."

"What about Judge Trapani?"

"He's a bad apple, that's for sure, and I've often heard it said you could buy him."

Tubby did not personally know about "buy," but he had once done a subtle arm-twist on Judge Carlo Trapani, and a client named Cesar Pitillero had miraculously gotten his sentence reduced. Pitillero was due out of state prison in three more months.

"Is that why you reported him to the Judiciary Commission?"

"Who said I did that?"

"You told me."

"I've got a big mouth. No, I reported him because he pulled a gun on me in my own chambers and said he'd blow my brains out."

"What for?" Tubby caught an errant slice of tomato from his sandwich before it hit the sidewalk.

"Because I told him I thought he was a crook. One thing led to another. I never had anything real on him. And even if I did, Marcus Dementhe did not seem to be too interested in Trapani. He's after the other guys."

"If they aren't doing anything wrong, then you don't have anything to trade."

"That's right. So I guess my goose is cooked."

"Not necessarily. You were definitely set up."

"What?" The judge's voice was loud enough to

make a curious antelope prance away and the kid who was about to feed it a peanut start to cry.

"I talked to Sultana, Al. How shall I put this? She was paid to come on to you."

"Paid? Like with money? By whom?"

"Apparently a man named Max Finn. He paid her to go to the party at Lucky LaFrene's house, with instructions to cozy up to you."

"That's unbelievable."

"I know it must be a blow to your ego, man. If it makes you feel any better, she says she has developed a real fondness for you."

The judge's mouth fell open. He mopped his brow with a paper napkin.

"Do you happen to know that Max person?" Tubby asked.

"I never heard of him."

"Too bad, because I never heard of him, either, before this week. Then the son of a bitch dies on us. You might have seen it in this week's papers."

Hughes shook his head.

"So that's one promising lead that has disappeared. The really weird thing is, Max Finn was married to a woman I know, Norella Peruna. She claims to know nothing about her husband's line of work, which to my mind would be called pimping."

Hughes wasn't listening. He was watching an old Galápagos turtle climb on top of another one.

"She was paid to pretend to like me?" He was indignant. "But now she says she has . . . what was her word?"

"She's fond of you."

"Holy Jesus."

"She wants to help if she can, but she's also afraid of the DA."

"Why did they pick me?"

"Maybe because you're an unsuspecting target."

"Which is to say, dumb."

"Could be. Maybe *naive* would be a better word."

"What do you think we should do?"

"Keep hanging tough. Dementhe didn't give me a deadline. He may just want you to wiggle and squirm. If he calls me, I'll stall. Meanwhile, have you thought about telling the missus? Confession is good for the soul, they say."

The noise the judge made could be called a growl, and he glared at his lawyer.

"Just a thought, Al. Let me keep working on who put Sultana up to this and why. If we figure that out, maybe you'll get your life back. Only problem is, I can't find her. She hasn't called you, has she?"

"Of course not."

"Well, she picked a bad time to go missing because she's already told all the bad stuff about you to a grand jury, but the only ones who heard her say she was paid to entrap you were me and Cherrylynn. By the way, have you got any money to pay me?"

Like two prairie creatures grazing on the same tuft of grass, the two lawyers put their heads together and got down to basics.

20

The apartment that Debbie Dubonnet shared with her husband and newborn was on Zimpel, near the universities. They rented the entire upstairs of a nice house with big windows overlooking the street. She came to the door with a finger to her lips.

"He just went to sleep," she whispered, meaning Arnaldo Bertrand, or Bat, as he was called.

Grandfather and daughter tiptoed up the stairs.

He peeked into the child's room and saw a small pink head poking out of a blue blanket. She waved him into the kitchen anxiously, afraid he might wake her papoose up.

"I think it's safe. We can talk in here," she said.

"Your house looks real nice," he complimented her, since it appeared that she had tidied up for his visit.

"Thanks." She was pleased that he had noticed. "Let's sit at the table. I'll just make us some coffee. What did you bring?"

"Scones, as promised." He gave her the bag. Tubby did not really care one way or the other about scones. They were not exactly a part of his culture. Still, all of his daughters loved them.

"Goody." She was elated.

"You look swell."

"I'm still too big." She handed him coffee in a white mug he recognized as a hand-me-down from her mother. "I haven't been sleeping much. Marcos and I take turns getting up at night, but I'm the only one who can feed him."

"Marcos is keeping up with school?"

"Pretty much. He studies in the library as much as possible just to have some peace and quiet." She sounded jealous. "I'll get some more help during his Thanksgiving break."

Tubby kept quiet.

"What are you doing for Thanksgiving?" she asked.

"Don't know yet," Tubby said hopefully. "What about you?"

"I guess go over to Mom's. She's invited everybody."

Tubby changed the subject. "And Bat? Is he doing okay?"

"Oh, he's just fantastic. He is sweet and happy and just so cute, I can hardly stand it."

"I hope he wakes up while I'm here."

"Do you have to leave soon?"

"Not really." He watched her spread lemon curd on

an orange-and-cranberry scone. He scooped up a small spoonful and sniffed at it.

"So," said Debbie, sipping her coffee, "was there anything special you wanted to talk to me about?"

"Not really. I just wanted to see you."

"Overweight me."

"You look very trim. I did have one question, though."

She raised her eyebrows.

"You know, when you got Buddy Holly, that preacher from Mississippi, to come here to help with your wedding . . ."

"Of course."

"I was just wondering, how did you get to know him?"

Debbie took her time swallowing a bit of scone before she answered.

"He has a church in Bay St. Louis. I met him over there."

"I've been to the place. They said you had stayed there, but they didn't say why. I thought I should ask you."

"It was last spring. No big deal. I just needed to chill out. I kind of bumped into those guys. It seems a long time ago now."

He waited for about a minute, concentrating on his coffee, but she did not add any details.

"If you don't want to tell me about it, I guess I can understand. But the place, you now, is for homeless kids with drug problems and stuff like that. I didn't know you were there. I didn't even know you had any problems. I'm concerned, that's all.''

''It wasn't drugs, I just went through a bad time.'' She pulled at her bangs. ''I'm over it.''

''You won't tell me.''

''Daddy, what got me upset was I found out I was adopted.''

Her father's jaw dropped.

Debbie stared down at her half-eaten scone.

''You know, I never think about that anymore,'' Tubby said quietly.

She glanced at him, then away to the clock on the wall.

''Who told you?''

''Mom did. It came up when I told her I was pregnant. She thought maybe I should give my baby away, since I wasn't married yet.''

Tubby rubbed his forehead.

''It wasn't really a secret. We always meant to tell you, when you got older. And then it just never seemed very important. We both loved you very much, and we were a family, so . . . it never came up.''

''You should have told me.'' Her eyes were suddenly moist.

''What difference would it have made, really?''

''My God, Daddy, don't you think somebody should know who their parents are?''

''We are your true parents.''

''You know what I mean.''

''And you know what I mean. You change little

Bat's diapers and wipe his runny nose for a few years and see if you don't get pretty damned attached to him.''

"That's different. He came from my body.''

"That's an overrated connection, in my opinion. Look, I'm sorry you didn't hear it from us earlier. What else did your mother tell you?''

"Not much. That you took me from the hospital and that you don't even know where my biological mother is today.''

"That's true. I haven't even thought about your so-called biological mother in twenty years.''

"Did you know her?''

"I met her. She was pretty, like you. She was in high school and got pregnant and wasn't able to care for a child. I talked to her once or twice at the most. She was a nice kid.''

"Who was my father?''

"That hurts, kid. I'm your father. I was never introduced to the guy you're talking about. He probably had to sign something. I honestly don't remember. To me it never mattered.''

"You and Mom couldn't have a baby of your own?''

"At that time it didn't look like it.''

"What about Christine and Collette? Are they adopted too?''

"Did you ask your mother?''

"She said it was none of my business.''

"She may be right for once. Anyhow, I'd want to talk to them before I talked to you. Do you care?''

She thought about it.

"Not really,'' she said finally.

"So. You see why I don't care."

"I suppose, intellectually. I know you raised me and all, but it was just such a surprise. I mean, Mom says, 'You know, you're adopted,' and I'm like, 'What?' It was kind of weird, that's all. And I felt very bad. I kind of lost it. Some friends took me over to Biloxi for the weekend and when they came back I just stayed. I don't know what I was thinking about—maybe an abortion or maybe doing something to myself to hurt the baby. It only lasted a few days."

"That's when you met Buddy?"

"I remember I was sitting on a concrete bench looking at all the kids playing on the beach and feeling completely numb. He saw me and sat down. We talked and he conned me into going out to the farm with a promise of free food. Anyway, they were really nice, and I got over it and came home to Marcos and we decided to get married."

"You didn't tell me."

"Does that make us even?"

Tubby shook his head and reached across the table to grip her hand. Then they both stood up and hugged.

They were like that, sharing a good cry, when the baby started screaming and bouncing loudly in his crib.

"Duty calls," she said, rubbing her eyes on his sleeve.

"I've loved you from the first time I saw you," Tubby said hoarsely.

Debbie nodded and composed her face. She laughed.

"Life sure is funny," she said.
"If you're lucky," he said.
She led him into the bedroom.
"Look who's here, little boy. It's your grandpa."
The baby took one look and wailed.

21

"What's your vision of things, speaking spiritually?" Sapphire inquired, eyes wide.

Raisin had been around her long enough by now to know that this was a serious question. He swatted a bug on his jeans and tried to think of something relevant to say. His "vision" was off, never properly restored, in fact, since the rave concert.

A low, mournful ship's horn sounded somewhere on the river, and he craned his neck to try to see the vessel above the trees that lined the bank. He and Sapphire were sitting on the top of a grassy levee upriver from Hahnville. Behind them were endless fields of sugarcane. In front was a wet meadow, bearing signs of recent flooding, and the potential for a glorious sunset. Mosquitoes were a problem. They were attempting a picnic, complete with wine, cheese, and a crusty French loaf as long as a baseball bat. It had been Raisin's idea.

"Vision, let's see." Raisin groped for some good words. He hated questions like this.

"Can you give me a example of what you're talking about?" he asked finally in desperation. He intently studied the plastic cup of Cabernet Sauvignon in his hand.

"Sure, like for me, the universe is this great big wide-screen TV, with pictures that keep changing, you know, like when a computer is just sitting there with nobody using it and all these images of planets and deserts and blue skies just roll across the screen."

Raisin closed his eyes and tried to imagine, for a second, what she was talking about. "Yeah," he commented uncertainly.

"And it puts off an electrical charge. If you ever saw a biofeedback thing of your brain waves, that's what I mean. And you change the universe just with the way you change your thinking. You can get more serene, or more excited, and when you do the picture changes. When you cry it gets black or purple and scary and full of flying rocks, and—"

"You don't like the cheese?" Raisin asked.

She clenched her teeth. "That's just like you, trying to change the subject."

"No, it's just that we're out here having a picnic with a river, and a sunset, and you're talking about biofeedback machines."

"To me it's all connected. That was just an image anyway." She pouted.

"I'm sorry."

"The world around us is just a little piece of a much bigger thing, you know."

"Sure. I know that."

She lay back and put her head in his lap. Her finger traced a cloud.

"When you were younger, Raisin . . ." She paused. He winced. "Did you ever take LSD?"

"Why, sure," he said. He did not think she believed him.

"Did you ever go to rock and roll concerts? Or get naked and run through the woods? Or count all the ants in an anthill?"

"When I was younger, baby, my biggest concern was trying to keep my ass from getting shot off in a rice paddy."

"That seems like such a long time ago." Her voice had a dreamy quality. Her hair was the color of clover honey, and her face was as innocent as a blue sky.

"Uh-huh."

"When I make music, I can sometimes imagine things like wars and bombs, but I'd rather go to other places. Places where people are trying to fill in the blanks in their lives and to love each other."

Raisin bent over to kiss her lips, but she turned away.

"You're not going to be around for a long time, are you," she said. It was a statement. She picked a blade of grass and twisted it around her fingers.

A little later, when they were packing up and loading stuff into the car, she told him that the picnic had been a nice date. In the twilight Raisin felt more lonesome than he could ever remember.

There is a hole-in-the-wall tavern behind Moskowitz Memorial Laboratory where doctors and nurses can drown their troubles after work. Flowers found Todd Murphy in a dark corner, playing pinball by himself.

''That machine's a real bitch,'' he said companionably when Murphy tilted out.

Murphy looked up and grinned. His black plastic glasses slid down his nose. He was surprised to have somebody to talk to.

''You work for the coroner. Am I right?''

''I'm an assistant,'' Murphy slurred. He raised an empty glass as if it was his excuse.

''Yeah. I think we met before. My name is Flowers. You told me some interesting stories about the bodies you cut up and all. Can I buy you a beer?''

22

Tubby was dreaming about Faye Sylvester. For some reason they were driving together on a winding road in Mississippi. He knew it was Mississippi because of all the pine trees and crows. Unexpectedly they entered the scenic perimeter of what apparently was a vast chemical plant. To his right, into the forest, a sign pointed the way to GATE 5. HYDROCHLORIC POLYMERS. AUTHORIZED ENTRY ONLY, it added. Tubby had the uncomfortable sense that his movements were being recorded by a camera somewhere and he slowed down. A Jeep was trailing behind him.

He was reaching for his security in the glove box when suddenly Faye and he emerged from the restricted compound into open farmland. The Jeep turned off into the woods.

The telephone rang.

"Tubby, help me," a hysterical voice sobbed.

"Norella, is that you?" Tubby struggled to wake up.

The sounds of metal clanging and men shouting orders came from somewhere in Norella's world.

"Yes, of course. I am in jail. These pigs have arrested me."

"What for?" he asked, sitting up in bed.

"They say I was trying to leave the country. They put some drugs in my luggage. It is called a frame-up, I think."

"Where exactly was this?"

"At the airport. You think the zoo?"

"But what were you doing there?"

"I was taking a trip!" she screamed. "Come get me out of here now!"

"Okay, have they set your bail?"

"How do I know? This place is disgusting. It's crowded and dirty!" she shrieked.

"Let me speak to somebody in charge."

"There is nobody in charge. I am on a pay phone. There are other women in here with me. They are prisoners, too, just like me. They gave us wet tuna-fish sandwiches to eat." She bawled.

"Well, just calm down. Get off the phone. I'll find out what's going on and get you out as soon as I can."

"I want you to sue them all," she proclaimed fiercely, and Tubby hung up.

He dialed Central Lockup and got put on hold. He thought about carrying the phone downstairs and fixing himself a drink. He could justify it. He had made five weeks without any booze. Who else could say that? It would be okay to start tomorrow. According to his watch it was already tomorrow. Tubby was struggling, soberly, with this when a tired voice said, "Jail."

"You've got a prisoner named Norella Peruna Finn. Can you tell me what her bail is and what's the charge?"

Back on hold Tubby started toward the stairs.

"Possession of a controlled substance and attempted flight from the jurisdiction. No bail yet. She'll go over to see the magistrate in a couple of hours."

"What time will it be when she gets back?"

"Sometimes it's ten o'clock."

"I guess I'll see you then."

The guard hung up, and Tubby went back to bed.

Properly outfitted in a navy three-piece suit and black wingtip shoes, Tubby Dubonnet presented himself in the courtroom of Magistrate Hampson at eight-thirty. It was one place in the building where lawyers were over-whelmingly outnumbered by civilians, all manner of them, bleary with lack of sleep, some cowed, some made belligerent by the sights and smells, disinfectants and discomforts, of their past few hours in a jail cell. Most wore orange jumpsuits with OPP stenciled across their chests.

The magistrate plowed through most of it by rote, in a practiced monotone. DWI? Bail $250. Armed robbery? Bail is $25,000.

Norella, slumped in a pew with a hand covering her eyes, was waiting her turn with the mostly male congregation. Tubby tried to get her attention by waving, but she wouldn't look up. Finally he prevailed upon a well-endowed police officer to tap his client on the shoulder. She jumped and her eyes followed the pointing finger to her attorney. He motioned for her to join him at the barricade.

Norella looked past the policewoman's blue chest to see who might object. Since no one was paying attention, she stood up, shook out her orange jumpsuit, and came to him with as much dignity as possible—difficult considering that her suit was at least five sizes too large and was bunched in comic cuffs around her elbows and ankles.

"I am not so attractive, am I?" she inquired sheepishly.

"Actually, orange pajamas look good on you," he told her. "Have you been before the judge yet?"

"No, I have just been waiting."

"Have they treated you all right?"

"I could not sleep. Everything here smells like roach spray. When can I go home?"

"That's what I'm here to find out. Who arrested you?"

"That man over there." She pointed out a square-headed detective wearing a baggy gray suit in the back of the courtroom. Tubby recognized him as LaBoeuf Kronke, who had been in charge at the boathouse the day of Max Finn's death. Kronke smiled at Tubby and wiggled an index finger at him by way of saying hello.

"Go back to your seat, dear," he instructed Norella. "Let's see what's what."

Reluctantly she rejoined the accused while her lawyer approached the law.

"Good morning, Mr. Dubonnet. I'm surprised to see you here so early," Kronke said pleasantly.

"You arrest 'em, I come. What brings you down here for a bail hearing, Detective?"

"Considering that Mrs. Finn is presumably well connected and that she started screaming for a lawyer the moment we laid a hand on her, I thought you would probably show up. I didn't want the magistrate to get all confused and decide we didn't have any probable cause and maybe let her go home by herself."

"So don't be coy. What did she do?"

"Attempted to flee the jurisdiction—specifically on a jet to someplace I can't pronounce in South America."

"You may be speaking of Tegucigalpa in Honduras. That's Central America."

Kronke frowned and shook his head. "I was afraid this was going to be difficult," he said.

"Not at all. Why can't she leave New Orleans?"

"She's a material witness to a murder."

"Oh, come on. Nobody gets arrested for that. And did you say murder? I thought that was still an open question. How did you know she was taking a flight anyway?"

"I had her tailed."

"Why?" Tubby displayed indignation.

"I told you," Kronke said calmly. "She's a material witness."

"So you stopped her, which interfered with her civil rights, laying your entire department open to an enormous damage suit, not to mention the embarrassment to her of being tailed and arrested, and then what?"

"In her luggage we find two grams of cocaine."

"Come on. Nobody smuggles cocaine to South America."

"Central America."

"Right. It's obviously a mistake or a plant."

"*Plant* is a nasty word. Anyway, we got her."

"Fantastic. What do you want to do with her?"

"We want her to cooperate with us fully in the investigation of her husband's death. She has to know more than she's telling. Maybe she's involved. I don't know. In any case I want her to start talking. If that means keeping her in jail, so be it. The drug-possession charge is very troubling."

"I'll bet it is," Tubby said. "Enlighten me—what is your theory about Max Finn's death? I thought the coroner was calling it a suicide."

"That's not final or public. And I don't suppose you'd tell me where you heard that rumor."

"Does it matter?"

"The coroner's inquiry is supposed to be confidential until the report is released."

"Well, it doesn't sound like murder, does it? Swallowing gambling chips from a casino is not exactly poison."

"It doesn't sound like a suicide either. I demand to know the source of your information."

"Strange way to kill yourself, indeed," Tubby agreed, "but strange things happen, and this doesn't add up as a murder. There's lots of quicker and easier ways to off somebody, not to mention cheaper."

"It is interesting," Kronke admitted, "but the lady over there hasn't helped us at all."

"She probably doesn't know anything that would help you. Norella is not the world's brightest woman. If her husband was involved in something illegal, he wouldn't have told her in a million years."

"What makes you think he was involved in anything illegal?" Kronke pounced.

"I'm speculating. Isn't that what you're doing?" Tubby was hot.

"You say she's a dummy?" Kronke was doubtful.

"A fiery Latin. Lots of beauty but not many brains." He smiled at Norella across the room.

"Are you gentlemen ready?" Magistrate Hampson called from the bench.

Tubby looked around and realized that all of the prisoners except Norella had been processed and taken away. He had not realized that the judge was waiting for him and the policeman to work out a deal.

"Why don't I take her out of here on her own recognizance?" Tubby asked the detective.

"Looks bad. Should be maybe a hundred thousand dollars."

"I'll bring her to your office tomorrow for a talk."

"What's she going to tell us?"

"I can't promise what she'd say."

"That's not good enough for me."

"Gentlemen," the judge said again. He had a golf game waiting.

"Your Honor," Tubby said, standing and going forward. "I am Mrs. Finn's lawyer. This charge of leaving the jurisdiction is very unusual—especially since this woman's husband died last week in a case that is still under investigation and is not officially a murder. She is under no compulsion to stay in Louisiana or Orleans Parish. There's been no determination as to the cause of death.''

"There's a possession charge here," the magistrate said, studying his papers.

"Yes, sir, and I think it's bogus. But in any case, Your Honor, no probable cause to search."

"Incident to arrest," Detective Kronke growled.

"You have something to say, Detective?"

Sure he did, and spun his tale. Tubby argued some more. An assistant district attorney finally arrived to glance at the file and add her two cents' worth.

Magistrate Hampson finally held up his hands and said, "I am setting bail at five thousand dollars. The court will accept Mr. Dubonnet as the defendant's personal surety, if he wants the responsibility. Anybody want to argue about it, take it to the district judge. Mrs. Peruna Finn, you are not to leave Orleans Parish until Mr. Dubonnet gets everybody's permission, capiche?"

Mrs. Finn nodded sullenly.

It took two more hours to get her out. There were some forms for Tubby to sign, where he promised to fork over $5,000 if Norella skipped her court appearance. Mentally kicking himself, he scribbled his signature. The last thing Detective Kronke said was "Don't forget we want her to talk to us."

"Screw yourself," Tubby said, but he immediately regretted it. There was no sense aggravating the police.

The deputies carried Norella back to the jail to process her out. She was back in her traveling clothes, waiting for her paperwork to catch up, when Tubby found her again, still behind a barred door.

"Have you got money for a cab?" he asked.

"Cash? No!" she said angrily.

"Well, here's a twenty. Call me when you get home. I've, uh, got some business I must attend to back at the office."

She waved him away with a disgusted look and stamped her foot on the floor.

He hit the sidewalk and used a pay phone on Tulane Avenue to call Flowers. As usual he got the detective's recording.

"This is Tubby. It's about eleven o'clock. Norella Finn is going to be walking out of Central Lockup and looking for a cab to take her home. If you get this message, I want the lady followed. And stick with her until we talk. And by the way, there may be a police tail on her too."

23

It was about six o'clock when Flowers came to Tubby's office. Cherrylynn had left for the day, punctually. Had she known that the detective was coming she might have stayed late.

Tubby was staring out the window watching a tugboat flailing against the current, trying to park an oil tanker at the Piety Street wharf, when he heard the rap on his door and waved the six-foot-tall detective in.

"Am I messing up your dinner plans?" the lawyer asked, trying to be polite.

"Dinner? My day's just beginning. I'm spying on a ship captain up in St. Rose tonight to see what he sneaks on board."

"Contraband?"

"Girlfriend."

"That sounds like great sport. Wish I could join you."

"Better bring a flask. Oh, I forgot. You quit drinking, right?"

"Taking a breather is more like it." His gut tightened. "Take a seat. Let me tell you what I need. Actually, it's several things."

Flowers extracted his leather notebook and waited expectantly.

The winch creaked loudly, and the man on the dock stopped cranking the handle and listened.

The sounds of rigging clanging against the sailboat masts, a muffled motor of a small boat puttering through the yacht harbor without wake, and snatches of laughter from the bars across the water reached his ears.

"Whatcha waitin' for?" his partner hissed.

"It's noisy," he whispered back.

"Nobody's home. Crank that sucker down."

Slowly the man worked the winch and allowed the sleek racing boat to settle into the water.

"Wanna hear some noise, let's start this baby up," his partner suggested, being funny.

The man didn't reply but jumped lightly into the vessel while his partner on the dock grunted and pushed it out of the boathouse. Their plan was to tie it to their sixteen-foot ChrisCraft and tow it quietly past the long row of docked sailboats to an ancient dry dock and gas pump that was often out of business but was open for them on this particular night. There they would pop the ignition switch.

"Somebody is going to see us," his partner sang

cheerfully, securing the line and jumping into the smaller boat. He pushed the lever that made the inboard motor start purring.

"Just act naturally," the man called softly. He stayed at the wheel of the sleek vessel and steered while his partner pulled them across the harbor.

Lights burned inside a couple of the sailboats, but no one was on deck, as far as they could see. Two people leaned against a phone pole in the shadows—they might have been necking. There were not any other boats moving around.

In a few minutes they came alongside the rusty dry dock, advertised by an old Pure gas sign. They scrambled to get the boat tied off, and another man joined them there.

He got to work with locksmith's tools, and after ten fretful minutes he whispered, "All set!"

"Shall we get under way?" the first pirate asked.

The motor caught, and they quickly untied from the dock. They puttered away and crept past the Coast Guard station without any lights.

Once clear of the harbor, the captain pulled the twin throttles back, and the OmniMach HydroRocket blasted off like a Roman candle in the night.

"I was parked at the boat launch across the street from the Finns' boathouse, just like you told me," Flowers reported on the telephone. "It was right at midnight o'clock, but a few people were still putting in and taking out. These two guys in a pickup truck drive in and backed down the ramp. They put a little boat in the water, parked the truck, and pushed off. I didn't pay too much attention to them.''

"Okay.''

"Now I'm watching the boathouse with my infrareds and I see a little movement. I get out and cross the street, and sure enough, somebody's taking the race boat out of its shed. I sneak around some more, and guess who it is—the two guys from the pickup truck. They take the boat and tow it across the harbor to some place with a hoist where I'm thinking they're going to pick it out of the water again.

"So I hotfoot it back to the pickup truck to see the registration, but instead of a tag it has one of those New Orleans specials.''

"A handwritten sign saying license applied for?''

"You got it. But the dudes got back before I had time to break in. The same time they get back, the damn boat goes flying out across the lake and disappears.''

"Okay.''

"Since I couldn't go after the race boat, I followed the pickup truck. They drove out Veterans Boulevard and guess what?''

"What?''

"They parked that truck right at Lucky LaFrene's Chevrolet, Hyundai, Nissan, and Isuzu, take the trailer off, hook it up to a brand-new sports car, and shoot out of there.''

"Where did they go?''

"Well, right then I had some bad luck. One of Sheriff Lee's finest taps on my window to see why I'm lurking on the side of the road. By the time I convince him that I'm a licensed professional with every right to act suspicious my guys have disappeared into the night.''

''Lucky LaFrene's, huh?''

''Yeah. What do you make of it?''

''Sounds to me like Lucky LaFrene's got himself a new boat.''

''And a fast one.''

''What else can you accomplish tonight?''

''You tell me.''

''Go to bed.''

''I'm still working on your other project. I hope to have something to tell you tomorrow.''

Tubby hung up.

This case has more wrinkles than all the peas in Asia, he told himself, and tried to get back to sleep.

24

The call from the DA came sooner than Tubby had hoped. First Assistant Candy Canary delivered the message.

"We are presenting our case against Judge Hughes to the grand jury next week" was what she had called to say.

Tubby was perplexed. "If you want his cooperation, that's no way to get it," he protested.

"You are welcome to come down and discuss a guilty plea."

"But he's not guilty. I've interviewed your informant, Sultana Patel, and she will say that she was paid to make advances to the judge. He was entrapped."

"That was not the testimony she gave in her sworn affidavit, and she reiterated those same facts before the grand jury."

"What I'm saying is true. A man named Max Finn paid her."

"And who is this Finn?"

"A man who preys on women. He died last week under suspicious circumstances."

"Very convenient. I'm not inclined to believe your dead witness, and I don't believe it would make any difference if I did. Your client broke the law."

"Very doubtful. And I don't believe a grand jury will indict him when it hears Sultana Patel's full story."

"They have already heard enough from her."

"I must insist that you call her to testify again."

"That's my boss's call." She hesitated, as if taking instructions from someone offstage. "I feel certain that his position will be that her original testimony, before she was coached by you, is all that is needed for the grand jury's deliberations. Whatever new claims she wants to make can come out at the trial."

"By then his reputation will be ruined."

"Reputations are not our business, Mr. Dubonnet. Justice is. We've extended the olive branch to your judge."

"If there were genuine corruption in the bench, Judge Hughes would willingly cooperate to root it out. You wouldn't need to threaten him. But he doesn't know of any."

Odd sounds crossed the line, and Marcus Dementhe's voice boomed in Tubby's ear.

"No corruption? The stench from that courthouse fills the city. Those hypocritical men and women who wear the robes are filthy with deception. If you can't see that, you're as blind as the statute of justice."

"Sir, what I see is not important. What Judge Hughes sees is, and he has no idea what you want."

"Then he is chopped liver."

"Can you give us a little guidance, maybe? I mean, who is your real target?"

"Everyone who violates the public trust is my target, starting with Judge Hughes. And if you don't want to see his name in the headlines of every paper in town next week, you had better come to me with an offer and some real dirt."

Dementhe hung up, and when Tubby could get his fingers to loosen their grip, he did too.

25

What used to take shoe leather now took CD ROMs. Flowers had them all: *Skip Trace IV, You Can Run But You Can't Hide, Who's Who in the Known Universe,* and the *Phone Book Cross-Check,* to name just a few. He also subscribed to all the monthly updates.

Playing on the screen now was one of the most useful, a compendium of credit-bureau reports on most of the humans in the United States. There was a disclaimer on it warning users not to make any credit decisions based upon the information contained therein, because to do so would be a violation of federal law, but Flowers was not in the money-lending business.

He was finding quite a bit of information about Max Finn, but he wasn't sure how much of it was useful. The man had a bank balance that sometimes shot into the hundreds of thousands and sometimes plummeted to NSF. Right now he owed everybody in town, except he was dead, of course. He was maxed out and delinquent on his Visa, Discover, and MasterCard. He slow-paid like molasses, and at the time of his demise even his house note was late. Once upon a time he had owned a race boat, but now somebody had stolen that. In short, unless Finn kept his dough in a mattress, he was dead meat, dead broke.

A bum, in Flowers's opinion. Still, he had a handful of thousand-dollar gambling coins in his system when he died. The detective took a sip of coffee and wrote some questions in his notebook: *Who would profit from a bum's death? What did he know worth killing for? How do you make a man swallow big plastic casino chips? Why do you do that?*

Flowers was supposed to learn everything there was to know about Max Finn and to keep a close eye on Norella, the widow. He was killing two birds with one stone when he rapped softly on the door of Apartment 103 on Arabella Street. The place, the whole building, was pink, and there were plastic flamingoes in the yard.

She answered by cracking the door and looking at him through the chain.

"Hi," he said, giving her his big smile. "I'm Sanre Fueres, and I'm a private detective working for your lawyer, Tubby Dubonnet. He's asked me to talk to you."

"About what?" she asked suspiciously.

"The circumstances of your husband's death."

"Let's see some identification."

He flashed her a badge and a laminated card with his

picture on it. He had bought them both through a catalog.

"You can call Mr. Dubonnet and check. His number is 555-2122."

"That's okay," Norella said. "You've got a nice face." She unhooked the chain and stood aside to let him in.

All of the furniture was black leather and chrome. The walls were white.

"I'm sorry about the way it looks," she said, not really caring. "The apartment came furnished. I took it because I couldn't stand to be in my own house anymore. Isn't that terrible? It's going to be repossessed anyway. Can I get you a drink?"

She was playing with her hands, so he gave her something to do.

"Sure. Have you some coffee?"

"No, I'm afraid not."

"How about a Coke, then?"

"No, I think the only things I have are some red wine and ice water."

"A glass of ice water, please."

She wiggled away in a very short dress. Flowers admired the view. A small motor but lots of voltage was his thought.

He installed a listening device under the coffee table and sat down again on the sofa before she returned.

"I'm having wine," she announced, handing him a glass of water. She had forgotten to add any ice.

"Gracias," he said.

"De dónde es?"

"New Orleans," he replied. *"Mi mamá vino de México."*

"Yo soy hondureña," she said. *"De un pueblo pequeño llamado Mosapa."*

"Have you lived here long?"

"For ten years. I came looking for a husband, and when I finally find one he gets killed."

"So sorry," Flowers said, "but of course that's why I'm here."

"I'm glad you came." Her eyelashes fluttered.

"Your husband's death is very curious. Just like the police we are having a hard time figuring it out. What did your husband do for a living?"

"I could not tell you. That is what the police kept asking me too. He spent lots of money and bought me some nice presents. I never really cared. He never went to the office like most Americans. He told me he made investments." She sipped her wine and looked at the floor.

"Do you have his personal effects with you? His papers and books?"

"They're all over at my house—what used to be my house."

"You think I could go see them?"

"I've still got a key. Maybe I could show you around."

"That would be very good. Don't you have anything here?"

"Just the things he gave me." She displayed her left hand, which was loaded with big sparklers.

"Love letters? Stuff like that?"

"He didn't write much. Why do you want to see private things?"

"It stands to reason if you didn't kill your husband, somebody else did. I'm looking for clues. It's what I do."

She opened her mouth as if she was about to say something, then changed her mind and slugged back some wine.

"Who were some of your friends?"

"What's that mean? I've got lots of friends."

"How about Max? Did he have lots?"

"Max gambled. When he was winning, everybody was his friend."

"What about Lucky LaFrene?"

"That was mostly business, I think."

"What kind of business?"

"I told you I don't know. They went out a lot at night."

"You weren't curious?"

Norella finished her wine and crossed her legs the other way.

"Look, Mr. Detective. Max was good to me. He didn't like me to ask questions so I didn't. We got along. I've known lots of worse men."

"How long were you married to him?"

"It would have been a year next month. You want to go see our house now?"

"If it's convenient for you."

She stood up and adjusted her skirt.

"I've got to tell you," she said, "that place makes me feel lousy."

She put her hands around Flowers's neck, stood on her tiptoes, and kissed him on the mouth.

"I'm a married man," he lied.

"Too bad. Let's take your car. Mine's out of gas." She picked up her purse from a little table by the door. Then she changed her mind and put it back again. "We can go later," she said, and unbuttoned her blouse. Then she reached behind her back and unhooked her bra.

26

Ever since his wife left him, Lucky LaFrene spent his best evenings at home playing with his fish. He had a custom-built aquarium in his den, and it took up nearly a whole wall. He had a polka-dot boxfish, and a Indo-Pacific wrasse, and a pantherfish, but his passion was his school of yellow tangs, because they were so gaudy. He had collected twenty-three varieties. He fed them French bread and ground-up nutria that he caught in his backyard, which bordered the 17th Street Canal, and they all lived together just fine, which the books said they wouldn't do.

He could monkey with the electrolyte level in the water and fiddle with the filters for hours, but he got a chance to do it only once a week or so because mostly he was eating out or having a few drinks with his many pals. He felt guilty, though, because his fish needed him. Like Felix there, his boxfish, who had something brown and cruddy growing on her dorsal fin.

The telephone rang and Lucky reluctantly set aside the little net he was using to herd Felix out of the artificial reef. He picked up the receiver with annoyance.

"Playing with the fishies, you bizarre stooge?"

The voice made the color drain from his face, and he stood up so straight, it looked as if he might topple over backwards.

"Why are you calling me a name?" he whined.

"Because that's what you are. I called to remind you of that."

"I'm not talking to anybody, if that's what you want to know."

"Keep it that way or you'll be floating in your own fish tank."

"You don't need to say things like that. I'm—" The line went dead.

Lucky hung up the phone and pushed the set away like it was hot to the touch. Suddenly afraid, he stole a look over his shoulder and almost jumped out of his chair when he saw Felix's fish lips pressed against the glass. The little bitch was looking at him.

"One thing turned up I thought you ought to know about," Flowers told Tubby.

"What's that?" Tubby had the phone jammed between his shoulder and his ear while he worked in the kitchen. He was whipping up a celery-and-carrot cocktail in the new juicer he had just bought.

"Max Finn wrote a couple of checks, one for fifteen

hundred and one for five thousand, to Boaz Enterprises. Is that your friend Jason Boaz?''

Tubby sat down hard.

''What were they for?'' he asked.

''Can't say. Would you like me to ask him and find out?''

''No, I'll ask him myself.'' He bit off a piece of celery and chewed it thoughtfully.

27

It was supposed to be a festive occasion. Trying to make peace, Tubby had invited Raisin and Sapphire out to dinner at the State Street Café. He even called ahead to order a full bucket of boiled crabs, shrimp, crawfish, and potatoes. He was going to be big about it and extend the hand of friendship to his ol' buddy Raisin and the nymphet Sapphire.

Things got off to a bad start because, in Tubby's sober opinion, Raisin had been drinking all afternoon.

"Have you ever been here before?" Tubby asked Sapphire as he got her seated at a table by the window.

"Place smells like a bus station," Raisin said loudly, dropping into a chair across from his date.

Sapphire stuck out her tongue at him.

"Do you mean the smoke from the bar?" Tubby asked.

"Like an open latrine," Raisin finished his thought.

"Good shrimp, though," Tubby said hopefully. He

had been sampling the bucket while waiting for his guests.

"This used to be a steakhouse, didn't it?" Raisin waved his hand for a beer.

"Yeah, for years and years."

"Too bad it changed."

"Everything is quite fine," Sapphire said in a determined voice.

Tubby decided he liked her better in person than he had on the tape. She didn't seem like such a child after all.

"You live in the French Quarter, right?" he asked, making conversation.

"Uh-huh. On Burgundy Street. I hardly ever get uptown."

"Two beers," Raisin instructed the waitress who had appeared from the cloudy kitchen.

"Just a Barq's for me," Tubby said.

"Same here," Sapphire said.

"Doesn't matter. I'll drink 'em both." Raisin motioned the server away.

"You're a musician, aren't you?" Tubby went on.

"And a damned good one too," Raisin chimed in.

Tubby wasn't ready to give up yet. "What kind of music do you like to play?" he asked, fiddling with the salt shaker.

"Country, mostly. Some people say I sound like Shania Twain."

"Shania Twain is a hat act," Raisin said emphatically. "Country music these days is nothing but baby-faced adolescents with clear complexions and big hats.

Hat acts!'' he repeated, and looked around, daring some-one to disagree.

Sapphire gave him a cold glare. She let her silence take effect and then said very quietly, ''You're just try-ing to sound like an illiterate hillbilly. Why do you do that?''

''Because that's just what I am,'' Raisin crowed.

Tubby stared out the window at a white-haired gent across the street trying to get his car unlocked. The man kept dropping his keys.

''You're coming on like a bitter old drunk,'' Sap-phire said, looking away.

''That's right. And I'm going someplace else where bitter old drunks are appreciated.''

Raisin pushed back his chair and stood up. ''Some things were not meant to be,'' he informed Tubby. On his way out the door he grabbed a bottle of beer from the waitress's tray.

She brought the rest of the drinks to the table.

''Is he coming back?'' she asked politely.

Tubby said he didn't know.

''I hope not.'' Sapphire sighed. ''I'm pretty hun-gry,'' she told Tubby. ''Are you leaving, too, or can I have some of those crawfish?''

''Dig in, dear,'' he said. ''I'm delighted to have you for company.''

She did as she was told, and her host followed suit. Between mouthfuls they had a nice conversation about the direction country music was headed and whether New Orleans would ever produce any greats in that field.

Raisin was a forgotten blight. Tubby bent Sapphire's

ear about all the great music you used to be able to hear around town, but then the waitress toddled up and said he had a phone call at the bar.

"Pardon me," he excused himself, thinking that Raisin was probably trying to horn back in. He found the telephone on the wall beside a video poker machine.

"You told me to call if something interesting happened," Flowers said excitedly.

"What's up?" Tubby asked, forgetting about the quarter he had automatically stuck in the game.

"Your client, Norella Finn, has led me on a merry chase."

"Where are you?"

"Way out in the east by Lake St. Catherine. She was at her house, all nice and peacefully tucked in, when suddenly she comes running out the front door and jumps in her car real fast. She got out on the interstate and just kept going. She took the old road out of town and led me out here to the boondocks. It was just a lucky thing I had enough gas to stay with her, because I was expecting a quiet night. Right now she's at a fishing camp on the water and I'm in some bushes trying to stay out of sight. Guess what?"

"What?"

"There's about a fifty-foot speedboat identical to the one stolen from the Finns tied up to the dock."

Tubby mulled it over.

"I'm going to come out there," he said finally. "Tell me exactly where you are."

Flowers did, and as Sapphire watched from her table the lawyer took notes on a bar coaster.

When he had hung up and returned, she arched her head inquiringly.

"I'm going to have to leave," he reported sadly. He really was sorry. "It has to do with a case I'm working on."

"Want some company?"

"I'd love it," he said, "but this might be a little dangerous and it's out of your way. I'm going down by the Rigolets."

"I hope you'll be all right," she whispered theatrically.

"Don't worry about me." He stood up. "You finish your meal. I'll go get the check." He went to find the waitress, but when he got back Sapphire was packed and ready to leave.

"I'll go with you." Without waiting for permission she led the way outside into the warm air of the evening.

"I can't take you," he said, catching up with her by his car.

"Hey, guy, you got me all revved up, you're not going to leave me like this."

"I'm afraid I'm going to have to."

"No way. I don't have a car or anything."

"I'll give you some cab money."

"Hell, I like excitement. I've already been dumped by one date, and I don't intend to be dumped by another. I'm not working tonight. So unless you're as big a jerk as your buddy, I'll just come along for the ride."

28

Not many roads are blacker and lonelier after dark than Highway 90, traveling east out of New Orleans. It is long and straight with nothing for scenery but dense cypress swamps and jagged stands of pine, ebony against a gray sky. Where the water touches land, fishing camps with colorful names, owned by weekenders and old salts who keep to themselves, perch precariously on crooked pilings driven into the marsh or the flat black sea itself. When the weather is calm and warm, as it was this night, the only ripples on the water's glassy surface are wakes from occasional small boats running far from the shore without lights, out for late-night sport or on errands of a private nature.

Tubby and Sapphire had discussed much as they raced through the uninhabited grassland—about what he did for a living and what she thought about the President—but he fell silent when they crossed the narrow Rigolets bridge, and she followed suit. At the sign that said ENTERING ST. TAMMANY PARISH, LOUISIANA, Tubby slowed down and began to clock the tenths of a mile as Flowers had instructed. The car was barely crawling when, about where Tubby expected, he spied the detective's blue Explorer nestled in some palmetto bushes beside the road. He eased his Chrysler onto the clamshell shoulder and parked beside the truck. He cut the lights.

"Wait here," he told Sapphire, and quietly opened his door. The smell of salt air and decaying marsh blew into the car. Somewhere tree toads without number sang, and far away a radio played a Beatles song.

A shadow stretched across the highway, and Flowers appeared from the bushes.

"We got some mosquitoes out here," he complained. "Who's that in the car?"

"Sapphire Serena. I was having dinner with her when you called."

"She's going to stay in the car?"

"I hope so. What's going on?"

"There's a camp down that little drive called the Red Saloon. Norella drove in about an hour and a half ago. Everybody seems to be in the building that's up on stilts. At least they were there a few minutes ago. I don't know who all is inside, but one of them is definitely Lucky LaFrene."

"Really?"

"I got a good look at him when he came onto the porch to take a whiz off the rail."

"You'd think he'd use the head inside."

"Maybe he likes nature. I've been hearing loud voices, but I haven't tried to get close enough to see what they're talking about. The racing boat is tied up to the dock, and there's another little motorboat down there somewhere too.''

Tubby swatted an insect on his wrist.

''Maybe we should just stay out here and see what they do,'' he suggested.

He swatted another one on his neck.

''You're the boss,'' Flowers conceded.

''But since I came this far I guess we'll just crash the party.''

Quietly the two men tiptoed through the saw grass and around the scrub brush that covered the land side of the camp. The moon rose gradually above the horizon, casting sharp shadows across their path.

The rustic house was raised up on pilings, and a wide deck wrapped around it. Hiding under the creo-soted poles, the two men caught their breath.

Suddenly, a pistol shot crashed through the air, and Flowers grabbed Tubby in a suffocating bear hug and wrestled him to the ground. Tubby struggled free and, sputtering, brushed the sand off his face.

''What the hell are you doing?'' he hissed at Flow-ers.

''Protecting the boss, boss.''

''You almost broke my back. I'm going up there and look in the window.''

Tubby crept to the wind-beaten wooden steps and started up, trying not to make a sound.

Flowers came behind him. A light shone through a window on the porch, and Tubby cautiously peeked in-side.

There was a body on the floor, almost centered on an oval rug. He recognized Norella Finn.

He yelped involuntarily when a hand grabbed his elbow, and Sapphire whispered, "What happened?" in his ear.

"What are you doing here?" Tubby gasped, but she ignored him.

Flowers signaled that he was going around to the back of the house, and he followed the porch around the corner.

Right away a loud grunt came from the general direction in which he had gone, followed by a thump.

Tubby and Sapphire exchanged glances, then watched as Lucky LaFrene—cotton-candy hair in place—stepped around the corner. He had a large pistol in his hand, and he wasn't smiling.

"Kind of scared me, sneaking up like that," he said. "I guess I'll have to ask you to come inside." He pointed the gun at Tubby's middle.

"No problem here," Tubby said, and Sapphire followed his lead.

They had to step over Flowers, who was spread-eagle on the deck.

"I had to tap him with my fish knocker," LaFrene said, indicating a bat lying beside the door. "Shouldn't surprise a man in the dark."

When they walked into the house they got another surprise. Norella was sitting up on the rug glaring at them.

"You aren't shot," Tubby said, stating the obvious. "Mind telling me what's going on?"

"I was practicing my own death," Norella said crossly.

"I'm afraid you interrupted the ol' gal's suicide," LaFrene said. "Why don't you sit down where I can keep an eye on you. You, too, miss."

Tubby and Sapphire squeezed together into a cheap plastic love seat made for juvenile guests.

"Why are you committing suicide?" Sapphire was concerned.

"Who is she?" Norella asked.

"A friend of mine," Tubby said. He was going to add, She's a woman your husband hit on, but he didn't know how that would go over. He listened hopefully for sounds that Flowers might be coming back to life.

"Because I want to disappear," Norella said angrily.

"Already wrote the fare-thee-well note," LaFrene added. He was the only one standing. "A note on the table, a gun with a bullet missing on the porch, and it looks like she fell into the water. The tide comes in and out, you know, and it's hard to find a body out there. It's the crème de la crime."

"Why are you disappearing?" Tubby asked.

"We're leaving here tonight on the speedboat," LaFrene said thoughtfully. "It's too hot to trot in this burg."

"What are you afraid of?"

"The same man you are, pilgrim, Marcus Dementhe."

"Yeah? Why?"

"That guy is the monster mash, I'm telling you. He'll snap me in two like a fire pole. I know too much."

"About what?" Tubby asked, watching the pistol droop in LaFrene's palm.

"I'll tell you a little something," LaFrene said, "since we're out here in the void of paradise. That crazy Dementhe killed Max Finn."

Tubby forgot about escaping.

"How's that?" He was all ears.

"I'll tell it just like it was. I told him, it ain't right. You owe me the money."

"It ain't right. You owe me the money!" Lucky LaFrene pleaded with Max Finn.

They were in the main room of the boathouse, half den and half kitchen, divided by a bar. Max Finn was sitting on his stool, building a tepee with plastic forks. Lucky LaFrene alternately paced around the kitchen and plunked down next to Finn, trying to get his attention.

"This shouldn't be hard to understand," Lucky said. He was trying to be reasonable. "I lend money to you, my pal, and my palomino pays me back."

Finn knocked his plastic forks into a heap and for entertainment began slapping his knees like bongo drums.

"Be serious for Chrissake," LaFrene begged. "This is not funny."

"Wrong. It's very funny," Finn told him.

"I want the papers on the boat," LaFrene said.

"Even with that you'll still owe me more than twenty-five thousand."

"Man, that boat is worth way more than I owe you. It's a collector's item. And you can't have it anyway."

"No, sir, Max. I want the boat. Give me the papers. Afterwards, we get it appraised and we can work something out for the difference. You owe me."

Max grinned at him. *"I can't find the papers,"* he said smugly.

LaFrene was out of patience.

"Max, I know it was you sent those guys to talk to me, but I need my moola. I want that boat!" He slammed his fist down on the bar.

Finn reacted by bouncing off his stool and crashing around his boathouse. He started tearing pictures off the wall and kicking the Mexican statues and ashtrays off the tables.

"You want this, Shylock?" he screamed, smashing a candlestick onto the floor. *"How about this?"* He kicked the television.

LaFrene watched speechless.

"You're crazier than a kettle of radishes," he whispered.

"You want this?" Finn held up a framed display of fifteen gold-plated gambling chips from a casino. LaFrene knew exactly what they were—thousand-dollar chips for the *"Fort Knox Megaslot Machine for the Twenty-First Century."* Lucky had been with Finn the night he won them. Since they also commemorated the fifteen ways Finn knew how to screw people, and since he had won plenty more that night, Finn had framed the

chips and put them on the wall where he could tell peo-
ple what a cool dude he was.

He slammed the case to the floor and jumped on it
with both feet.

"Hell, yes, I want that," LaFrene said, getting up.
"That's fifteen grand."

"Well, come and get them," Finn invited coyly. He
scooped the chips off the floor and shook off the glass.
Then he placed them on his tongue, one by one.

"Tastes great." Gulp.

"Like caviar, Lucky," Gulp.

LaFrene sat down heavily on his stool.

"You're a lunatic, Max," he said sadly.

The doorbell rang.

Max swallowed his last chip and looked around at
the mess he had made.

"I hope that's the cleaning lady," he said, and
burped. Stepping around an overturned lamp he went to
open the door.

"This is quite an honor." He stood back to let the
visitor enter.

Dementhe closed the door behind him and looked
past Max to take in the room.

"Hello," he said to Lucky, who nodded.

"Please get the obnoxious and disgusting grin off
your face, Max," he said to Finn.

Finn's smile stayed put. Dementhe's face turned red
and he jabbed Finn in the stomach with two stiff fingers
to make his point. When Max just opened his mouth, the
man jabbed him again.

"Eeeee," Finn wheezed. He clutched his throat.

"What's wrong with this fool?" Dementhe asked
LaFrene.

"He needs a head shrimper," Lucky said, but by
then it was too late for Finn.

*He was twirling slowly, gasping loudly, and beating
himself on the chest. He staggered toward the bar and
pointed a finger at Lucky, then, with a mystified expression on his distorted face, he pitched headfirst to the
floor.*

LaFrene held up his hands like he was under arrest.

"What did you do to him?" Dementhe demanded,
checking for a pulse.

*Neither one liked the odds, and they got out of there
fast.*

"I don't know if that's actually a murder," Tubby said
when he had listened to the story.

LaFrene shrugged. "In my opinion it was. He was
desiring to kill poor Max, except Max died on his own.
Give Dementhe time, and he'll do the same to me and
this little lady right here." He pointed at Norella, who
was checking her appearance in the chrome legs of the
coffee table. "I'm doing this for love, doll," he called,
and blew her a kiss.

She checked the mole under her ear.

"Why would Dementhe want Max Finn dead?"

"Because they was cooked up together in some
crazy scheme. I don't know the details. It had to do with
Max's call girls and how they was going to frame all the
judges. Something screwed up, is all I know."

"I guess it did," Sapphire said, jaw squared.

"What's your pointed view, little damsel?" LaFrene asked.

"I'm just one of the call girls, mister, if you must know. Just one of the chicks who flittered into his tree."

Intrigued, LaFrene said, "It's bees who flitter through the trees, doll. Have you got a stinger or are you a humdinger?"

"I can hum, and I can sing too. Despite what Max Finn did to me."

"He was a crooked pot of piss, that's no lie."

"To me he's like rain in the sky, but he'll be gone by and by."

Tubby's head had been snapping back and forth, trying to follow this exchange, but, hopelessly puzzled, he interrupted.

"What's Dementhe got against judges?" he asked. "Do you know?"

"Who the hell knows?" LaFrene spread his hands. "He's just a nasty man. Some people are like that. I knew him from grade school. Before he got religion he was a good guy. But I didn't get to be a lucky man waiting for the knife to fall. We're clearing out. Norella, are all your bagatelles packed?"

"They're all in the boat," she said, avoiding Tubby's eyes.

"Okay, you go first out the door, and be careful that fellow out there is still sleeping. You should drop your good-bye note on the coffee table on the way."

Norella placed a folded piece of paper under an ashtray. She passed Tubby and Sapphire without looking at them and slipped out the door.

"Exactly where is everybody going?" Tubby asked, making conversation.

"We're going to make an island off Texas," LaFrene explained. "It's a real nice place to stay for a while, where nobody bothers you. Kind of romantic, I thought. A lovely spot for me and my Queen of Denial. Now the plan has to change."

"Are you going to kill us?" Sapphire asked.

LaFrene tugged on his earlobe like he was giving the matter some thought.

Tubby's eyes did not leave the gun.

"It's up to you. I ain't a bad rapper. I'll take you along if you want, my dear. I'll even take your attorney and counselor-at-law buddy. It would be a vacation," he said, warming to the subject. "Like de owl and de putty-tat, we'll sail away for a year and a day. Of course, if you don't want to go, it's hello fishies for you."

Sapphire nodded. A vacation sounded good to her.

"I would love a trip myself," Tubby assured him. "What about my man out on the deck? Can we take him too?"

"I think we ought to." LaFrene's eyes wiggled. "If you can lift him into the boat. But if you try anything funny, I'll plug all three of you to the kingdom of zydeco."

With LaFrene behind them they went out onto the deck. The black sky was full of stars. There was a breeze, but the moon had hidden behind a cloud.

LaFrene showed them the narrow steps that led down to the long speedboat moored below.

"We're going to have company," LaFrene called to Norella. "When they see how much fun we're having, they'll never want to leave."

Tubby bent down to check on Flowers, who was breathing softly, and he motioned for Sapphire to help him.

"I think he's going to shoot us once we're out in the Gulf," he whispered to the girl.

"His aura is green," she agreed.

"Grab your buddy and let's move it quick," LaFrene instructed.

"And I mean real quick," he said much louder. Cars with blue lights flashing were bounding down the driveway toward the camp. Overhead, a helicopter approached at high speed, raking the ground with a spotlight.

"Jump in!" LaFrene commanded, pushing the gun into Tubby's face but watching the sky. "That bastard Dementhe will surely kill us all."

Tubby put a hand on Sapphire and flung her down the steps toward the boat.

"Leave him. Leave him," LaFrene told Tubby, and pushed him away from Flowers.

He jumped into the boat, where Norella was huddled with her hands over her ears. LaFrene threw off the ropes and leapt in beside them. Tubby had a chance to take him then but tripped over Sapphire's foot and sprawled onto the fiberglass deck. LaFrene ignored the commotion and dashed to the controls. The twin gasoline engines exploded into life, and with a great swerve that threw all three passengers into a heap, the OmniMach HydroRocket roared away from the dock. Loud voices, footsteps, and gunshots punctuated their departure. The helicopter in the black sky wheeled about and pursued them.

"Now we're cruising," LaFrene screamed as the mighty boat planed out and flew across the Intracoastal Waterway toward Lake Borgne.

"Holy shit, this thing can fly," Tubby exclaimed, disentangling himself from Norella. He slid beside Sapphire and together they got on their knees and raised their heads high enough to see the water flashing by.

The shoreline whipped past, and in the distance was a beacon that Tubby judged to be the lighthouse at the Rigolets. The helicopter passed low overhead, and they were momentarily caught in its beam.

"Surrender, or we shoot you out of the water!" boomed a voice from a bullhorn. The voice could belong to the district attorney himself.

"Catch us if you can, big guy!" LaFrene cried, having a great time. The craft accelerated.

Up ahead other boats appeared, red lights flashing over the water.

"They're blocking the way," Tubby yelled into Sapphire's ear. He stumbled forward and shook LaFrene's shoulder, pointing at the blockade ahead.

"You'll have to stop," he screamed.

"In a pig's ear!" LaFrene cried. He was grinning as wide as a mouth can grin, and the two boats converging across their bow were getting closer quick.

Tubby turned around and fell back on Sapphire. Unaccountably, she was laughing too. "He's nuts," Tubby told her.

"This is really fast." Her teeth chattered.

Flashes from the helicopter above indicated that someone was shooting at them.

Rigid by LaFrene's knees, Norella caught her lawyer's eye and made the sign of the cross.

"Can you swim?" Tubby shouted at Sapphire.

"Not well!"

"You want to get shot at anymore?"

"Not much!"

"Hold on to me!"

She nodded her head vigorously, and arm in arm they got to their feet and jumped over the side of the boat.

The water hurt when they hit it and slid along it, and for a minute they were separated and both lost in the wake and froth churned up by the fleeing speedboat.

"Here I am," Sapphire sputtered, and Tubby dog-paddled over to her. To keep from sinking he kicked off his ninety-dollar sneakers.

"This way," he gurgled, and they swam in the direction of a dark marsh a hundred yards away. It took a long time to get there, and they floated on their backs, looking at the moon. About the time they reached the grass, a great explosion ripped the sky—the lights coming before the sound. The crack was followed by several smaller booms, but Sapphire and Tubby could not see what had happened.

They felt mud underfoot. It was thick and deep, and

for a half an hour that seemed like forever they crawled
and swam and dragged themselves through the grass and
gook until miraculously they came upon earth solid
enough to support their weight.

Exhausted, Tubby lay in the weeds, looking at the
stars. Sapphire fell down beside him. They were too tired
to talk.

Finally, Tubby got up and scouted around. He found
an old-fashioned rabbit trap made out of a wooden box,
so he figured their little island in the marsh might be
attached to dry land, at least in the morning at low tide.
He also found a rude lean-to made of rusty sheet metal,
perhaps a car hood or the hull of a sunken boat, and the
remains of a campfire. He reported back to Sapphire and
helped her limp to the shelter he had found.

"Too bad we don't have matches for a fire," he
said.

"What about this?" she asked, producing a dispos-
able lighter from her jeans. She flicked it, and it worked.

They couldn't find much to burn, just a few twigs
and a couple of broken planks and the rabbit trap, but the
small fire they made was very cheerful. It also illuminated them enough so that they could see how much
mud was caked on their bodies. Feet to the blaze, they
settled down on grass pillows, spirits improving.

"You picked the wrong night to get all revved up,"
Tubby said, picking the mud off his cheek.

"It's not so bad," she replied. "Do you think tomorrow we'll be able to find food?"

"I'm dreaming about a thick steak," he said.

"Who is this Dementhe person Lucky was talking about?"

"He's your district attorney, Sapphire. Don't you follow politics?"

"Oh, yeah, I think I heard of him." She paused. "Actually, politics don't make much of a difference to me."

"A friend of mine says New Orleans politics are too dirty for Tide."

"Is that your girlfriend?"

"Not really. No. What makes you ask that?"

"Just the way you said it, I guess."

"Well, her name is Faye. We're in different worlds. She's clean and upright and does good for people. I'm a sleazeball lawyer. She lives in the country, which I don't. I live in the city, and she's not interested. I don't think it's fated."

"I'm sort of in the same fix. Me and Raisin are not exactly on the same wavelength."

"He's different from most people, not just you."

"Tell me about him, please. He's been your friend for a long time, right?"

"We go way back."

"Vietnam bothers him a lot."

"Really? He hasn't mentioned it to me since I don't know when."

"You didn't go to war, did you?"

Tubby studied the moon. "No. That's another long story."

"But you're still friends?"

"Yeah. I forgave him for going and he forgave me for not going. It's all history now."

Sapphire snuggled under his arm.

"Some people are easy to be around," she said. "Your friend is a challenge."

"He's having a complicated battle with his moral center," Tubby opined.

Together they counted the stars. She sang a song.

"Like ivy clinging to the wall,
My love for you will never die.
Like stories that two lovers tell,
My tale and yours are a knot you tie.
I think of you each night
Till I fall asleep.
You keep me warm and hold me tight,
Even though I'm counting sheep.
Where are you, baby? Too far away.
My body's aching for a lay."

"Very pretty," Tubby said softly.

"I just made it up," she said.

They drifted in and out of sleep, picking up their conversation where they had last left it, then dozing off again.

Once she brought him awake by saying, "I think people are a lot like stars."

"What do you mean?"

"There are so many of them, but each one has its own special shine," she said dreamily. "You could never visit all of them, even if you were Mr. Spock. But some of them are still very special to you. Even when you can't see them because of the clouds in the sky, they're still special.''

Tubby started to slip away.

''And it's funny. People spend so much of their lives like editing out or something all the really beautiful things just so they can accomplish their little-bitty tasks.''

Tubby went to sleep.

Morning began with the sounds of birds. Ducks flew overhead in great number, announcing a thin pink beam of light across the eastern horizon. Tubby sat up, stiff and wet. Sapphire was rolled into a ball, her head wrapped in her arms. The grass all around them was covered with dew, but when Tubby stood up to stretch he felt strong and new.

''Is it daytime?'' Sapphire asked from under her elbow.

''It will be soon. Here comes the sun.''

She sat up to rub her eyes and watch. She ran her tongue around inside her mouth.

''Look, I think that's an eagle,'' Tubby said, pointing to a dot in the brightening sky.

''I never saw one of those before, or those either.'' A flock of brown pelicans floated in a lazy line over the marsh.

''A lovely spot indeed,'' Tubby said. ''Now let's get out of here.''

They set off hiking, following animal trails through the grass.

''You know, Mr. Tubby,'' she said as they walked

through the woods, "I think we're going to be friends for a long time."

After an hour they popped up at Fort Pike. The sign said LOUISIANA STATE PARK, HOURS 9 TO 9, NO UNAUTHORIZED ENTRY, but they walked through the parking lot anyway. There was a pay phone by the ticket booth and, lo and behold, it gave them a dial tone.

Tubby called Cherrylynn first, and got her answering machine. He explained where he was and that he needed a ride, and that he was going to try to track down Raisin next.

"Call my apartment," Sapphire suggested. He did, and Raisin picked up the phone.

"Serena residence." The voice was groggy.

"Help," Tubby said. He told Raisin where to find them.

Another hour passed, during which Tubby and Sapphire enjoyed the Sunday morning watching cars and trucks rush up and down the highway.

Sapphire talked about the work she did and her dreams of being a country music star.

"Music may be your ticket out of here," he said, intending encouragement.

"Maybe. I've always lived in New Orleans, though. I might not know how to act anyplace else."

"I imagine you'd learn."

"I'm not sure I'd want to. I can just be me here, and people have to learn to live with me."

Then they were rescued. Raisin was driving his old Mazda, and Cherrylynn was the passenger. They had brought a thermos of coffee and a bag of McKenzie's doughnuts.

Soon after they were all packed in and headed back to New Orleans, they passed the turnoff to Lucky LaFrene's camp. Flowers's car was gone. So was Tubby's.

Raisin did not talk much along the way. Sapphire hummed, and Cherrylynn napped.

Back in New Orleans their first stop was Tubby's house. Raisin declined the invitation to come in, and Tubby was too worn out to press the point. Sapphire looked cross, but said she would go home with Raisin. They drove away, and Cherrylynn went with him inside.

"Would you mind checking my messages?" he asked her. "I've got to get in the shower."

He was standing in the spray and soaking up steam when Cherrylynn shouted outside the bathroom door, "The only message was from Flowers. He said he woke up with cops all around him but he managed to slip away. He's got his car but left yours. He says he has some news you should hear."

Restored and wearing clean clothes, Tubby watched her make coffee while he called Flowers back. He left a message, and soon his phone rang.

"You're alive," Flowers said.

"And so are you."

"With a lump on my head, yes."

Tubby told him about spending the night in the

marsh and repeated Lucky LaFrene's story about the death of Max Finn.

"Maybe I should go talk to my friend the coroner's assistant and see if that account is consistent with the way Finn died."

"Don't drop the name Dementhe."

"Hell, no."

"Because the man is dangerous."

"Sure. Maybe I should ask him if any unidentified women have shown up, because I still can't find Sultana Patel."

"Yeah. And another thing you can ask him."

"What?"

"You told me that the coroner reported finding five thousand-dollar chips in Finn's gut."

"Uh-huh."

"According to LaFrene there should have been fifteen."

That afternoon, while Tubby was polishing off a dunning letter to Mandy Fernandez, and thinking about Ezra Brooks over ice, the phone rang. It was Flowers.

"Sultana Patel is dead," he said.

"Oh, no."

"There's something you should see. Can you meet me up on Burdette Street?"

"Sure."

Flowers told him the address. "Wear old clothes," he suggested. Tubby looked helplessly around the office

and decided he was stuck with the pressed suit he had
on.

Flowers was waiting for him behind the tinted windows
of his Explorer. Tubby got into the passenger seat and
closed the door.

"You see that house over there?" Flowers asked.
"Well, there's a man living underneath it. I found him
this afternoon. He may be a witness to Sultana's murder."

Flowers explained how the coroner had shown him
an unidentified corpse and how Flowers had given the
corpse a name. The detective had then come to this spot,
where the body had been discovered, to cover the ground
the police had missed.

"She was found right there beside the telephone
pole," he told Tubby. "She was there a couple of days
and nobody said anything."

Flowers had knocked on doors but gotten nowhere
until he caught Mr. Armstrong rocking on his porch.

"The only thing the old man would say was 'It's a
mighty hard world,' but he kept tipping his head toward
the house next door, like there was something funny
about the place. 'It ain't none of my business, but you
might look around underneath that house,' he told me.
So I did."

Crawling on hands and knees behind Flowers, Tubby
cursed silently. He was trying to keep from getting cut

on the rocks and glass and little bones when he encountered Purvis, hiding behind a tilted brick pier staring at the two intruders in terror.

"That ain't much of a witness," Tubby said to Flowers, brushing off his clothes. He couldn't get the stench of the crawl space out of his nose.

"He gave us a man and the color of the man's car. Maybe he could identify the man if he saw him again."

"Right. Imagine how he'd look in court."

"You think we should call the city, or get him a doctor or something?"

"What the fuck do I know?" Tubby asked, disgusted. "Let's just get out of here."

Through her screen door Mrs. Chin watched the two strange men get in their van and drive away. She wondered what they were doing in this neighborhood.

At the Upperline the reflection of candles flickering in the windows and the quantity of booze in the drinks puts everything in a relaxing glow. Sapphire, Raisin, Cherrylynn, and Flowers were all Tubby's dinner guests. He was thanking everybody for their help. The first course was drinks, which everybody was enjoying except the host, who was sticking to ginger ale. The appetizers pleased him more, green fried tomatoes with shrimp remoulade and spicy shrimp with jalapeño corn bread.

And by the time plates of roast duck, garlic-crusted Gulf fish, and veal grillades with mushrooms, peppers, and cheddar grits had been passed around, the turmoil of the last few days was far from anybody's mind.

Those so inclined were embarking upon dessert when the door swung open, and a barrel-chested man entered. He came to their table.

"Good evening, Mr. Dubonnet," he said.

"Good evening, Officer Kronke," Tubby replied. "Would you join us for coffee?" He hoped the answer was no.

"I'm afraid not. I've got your car in the pound, Dubonnet. It was picked up on Highway Ninety, at a crime scene. Now I've got orders to pick you up for questioning."

Before Tubby could protest, Sapphire piped up with "Mr. Dubonnet had nothing to do with any crime. I was with him the whole time. You cops are the ones who ought to be questioned."

So Kronke picked her up too. Tubby did not want to create a riot at one of his favorite restaurants, especially with two uniformed policemen glowering though the window at him. He barely had time to toss Cherrylynn his American Express card on his way out the door.

"You have an arrest warrant for me?" Tubby asked when they got outside.

"It's like this," Kronke said earnestly. "I've got a subpoena requiring you to testify before a grand jury this afternoon. Which is now past tense. You didn't show up. So I can arrest you now."

"What subpoena? I never was served with any subpoena."

"I'm serving you now. Get the picture? You want to come with me in my car or go with them to get booked?" He pointed his chin at the two cops leaning against their patrol car.

Sapphire held Tubby's hand in the backseat of Detective Kronke's maroon sedan.

"This is like a police state," she complained. "I've seen this kind of stuff in the movies."

"There, there," Tubby consoled her. "Think of all the damages you'll collect for wrongful arrest."

"There's no arrest involved," Kronke said from the front seat. "You're coming with me voluntarily."

"Nobody's going to believe I left dessert sitting on the table at a first-class restaurant to go to the police station voluntarily."

"We're not going to the station."

"Where are you taking us?" Sapphire demanded, before Tubby could.

Kronke didn't answer. He cruised up Napoleon Avenue to Broad and over the interstate, but he passed the turnoff to the jail. Their destination was a white concrete building a few blocks away.

"Here we are," he said, pulling up to the curb marked LAW ENFORCEMENT VEHICLES ONLY. "You're so important, you rate a personal audience with Marcus Dementhe himself."

He held open the back door, and Sapphire got out, followed by Tubby.

"We don't have to talk to anybody, do we, Tubby?"

she asked angrily. They were crossing the lawn. Animals scurried under the bushes.

"No, I suppose we could leave," he said, glancing behind him at the dark, empty street, "but let's hear what the man has to say."

"See, I told you it was voluntary." Kronke chuckled, leading the way up the steps. He had a plastic card that made the doors open. They took an elevator to the top floor. The lights were on in the lobby, when they stepped out, and at the end of the hall the district attorney's door was open.

Marcus Dementhe was posed behind his desk, reading a stack of papers in blue binders by the light of a green lamp. Tubby waited at the door until he looked up.

"Come in, Mr. Dubonnet, and who is this with you?"

"I brought her along," Kronke explained, "because she said she was with Dubonnet last night."

"Very well." The voice was cream. "And what is your name?"

"Her name is Sapphire," Tubby said, "and what's the point of bringing us down here?"

"You are on the verge of being charged with several felonies, Counselor, including aiding and abetting an escaping murderer, and I am doing you the courtesy of questioning you first."

"Who escaped? What murderer?" Tubby fumed.

"Why don't you wait outside, Detective?" Dementhe instructed Kronke. "I'll call you if I need you."

Kronke departed and closed the door behind him.

"The accused murderer, won't you sit down, is a gentleman named Lucky LaFrene. The victim was a man named Max Finn. We believe Mr. LaFrene may also have killed your so-called client, Norella Finn, and faked her suicide, or else he may have run away with her. I don't know which."

"LaFrene escaped?"

"Yes, in a boat. He eluded officers detailed by my department. In the process two police department watercraft were destroyed. Luckily, no one was seriously hurt. Can you please explain for me why your car was parked on the highway near Mr. LaFrene's fishing camp?"

"Hey, I know you!" Sapphire interrupted.

The district attorney frowned at her.

"What's that button you've got on your coat?"

"It stands for Fully Reliant on God," Dementhe informed her.

"Yeah, I know you, Mr. Frog. You're the guy who raped me. It's you, all right," she said, leaning over his desk to put her face close to his. "You were a big buddy of Max Finn's back then. You could just hop right into bed with him and hump his girlfriend."

"I don't know what you're talking about," Dementhe said sternly.

"Sure. Let's hear you say 'Sweet Mary' a couple of times. I know your voice." She turned to Tubby triumphantly. "It's him, the guy who got into bed with me and Harrell or Finn or whatever his name was and made me have sex."

"This is preposterous!" Dementhe stood up and wagged his finger at Sapphire.

"Why, you holier-than-thou sonofabitch!" Tubby got between them. "You ought to be in jail yourself."

"Get out of here," Dementhe yelled.

"I'm going to sue you personally," Tubby yelled back. "Aiding and abetting something. I've got you now. You and Max Finn worked together, huh? What did you do, tell him to hire one of his girls to set up Judge Hughes, and then kill Finn to make him shut up about it? And did you kill Sultana, too, so she wouldn't talk?"

"I've never killed anybody, you idiot! She killed herself!"

"Oh, so it was you who dumped her body. Maybe it was a murder and maybe it wasn't, but, by God, it's your fault either way, and I'm enough of a Louisiana lawyer to know that if you cause any harm by your fault, you pay!"

"Out! Out!" Dementhe ranted.

"You're going to pay lots," Sapphire promised.

"Detective Kronke! Get these people out of here!"

Tubby offered his arm to Sapphire, and together they made their exit.

Kronke rode with them down the elevator.

"What did you do to make the old man blow his cork?" he asked.

"I'll tell you over dessert, Detective. If you can get me back to the restaurant quickly, my party may still be there. I think I have some information that will make your investigation much more productive."

* * *

Tubby's theories left Detective Kronke more than a little confused.

"You tell me Marcus Dementhe is 'responsible' for the death of Max Finn, but the coroner admits he doesn't know how the hell you force gambling chips down a man's throat. You say the DA is 'responsible' for the death of Sultana Patel, which the coroner has not even classified yet. You say my suicide of Norella Finn is not a suicide at all, but a woman terrorized into leaving the country by Marcus Dementhe. Is there any other crime you say the DA has committed?"

"He raped me," Sapphire said.

"Which you say happened when you were naked in bed with another man having consensual sex, and you know it was Marcus Dementhe because he has a button that says FROG on it—"

"That's the story," Tubby cut in. "Do what you want to with it. If the man does not have criminal liability, I bet I can still prove his civil liability for the damage he has caused to all of these victims."

"What you've got here is a murder case without a murder in it. This is not my department," Kronke said, and left, his coffee cup empty.

"You're going to sue him?" Sapphire asked.

"I don't know," the lawyer admitted. Sapphire's case was not so great, if you wanted to be objective about it, and further public inquiry into the deaths of Finn and Sultana would produce the very embarrassment that Al Hughes was trying to avoid.

"My first concern," he said, "would be to protect you."

"I'm pretty good at protecting myself," Sapphire said, sticking her lip out bravely. "I've got a lot of friends in this town."

Tubby asked Cherrylynn to come into his office the next morning for a private talk.

"I know I may not be the world's best boss," he told her after she sat down. "And lately I've just been, I don't know, mad at everything. So, I'm trying to say I can understand why you've not been very happy here. I'm going to try harder, and—"

"Mr. Dubonnet," Cherrylynn interrupted, "you're not the reason I've been unhappy."

"I'm not?" he asked in surprise. "Why, I thought—"

"No, I've been going through some stuff of my own. It's had nothing to do with you."

"Well, gee. I guess I'm relieved. Is there anything I can help you with? I would really like you to stay here, Cherrylynn. You're a big asset, is what I mean."

"Oh, I know that, Mr. Dubonnet. If you must know, I've been having some questions about my own sexuality. That's all. It was nothing to do with you."

Mouth open, Tubby just stared at her.

"And then Rusty, my old whatever, showed up and like an idiot I let him hang around for a few days, and then I thought I might be pregnant, but it turns out I'm not."

Tubby closed his mouth.

"I was very upset, of course, and then, you know, I

was listening to *The Bob Show* on the radio and there was this man on from the Louisiana Department of Revenue talking about how they had lots of unclaimed money and you just had to call their telephone number.''

She smiled for the first time, in weeks it seemed.

''Anyway, I called the number and gave them my name and, did I ever tell you I was married once?''

Tubby's brow furrowed. ''Of course. You eloped in the twelfth grade.''

''Right. Well, did you know he died? He got smashed in a car wreck in Dulac, right where you turn off to Cocodrie. Amazingly, he had a life insurance policy from his J. C. Penney credit card. The money was just sitting there because he spelled my name wrong. With the interest I'm supposed to get fifty-five thousand dollars.''

He returned her smile.

''Anyway, I think I'm getting some things resolved. I'm a little happier about myself and my job. I expect I'll stay around here for a while, if that's okay with you.''

''Why, sure. I don't know what else I can say.''

''Not a whole lot.'' She stood up. ''It's nice talking to you like this. Maybe we should do it more often.'' She beamed at him and left the room.

Stay tuned for the next installment, Tubby told himself. Clearly, I am not the center of the universe.

''I would like you to talk to the coroner again,'' Tubby told Flowers. ''What's his name?''

''Todd Murphy.''

"Tell him to get off the fence on Sultana Patel. Damn right she was murdered, and the murderer is Marcus Dementhe, but Murphy doesn't need to know that. Once he calls it a homicide, the police will get back on the case. I guarantee that they'll find some trace of her blood on him or in his car and that will be the final scandal for our DA."

"Sure, I can try, Tubby. I can't force him to make a decision, though."

"Yeah? Well, just remind him how fifteen chips went down Finn's throat and how, according to Murphy, only five came out."

"Okay, but what if Dementhe's, you know, thoroughly cleaned the car he used to carry Sultana's body?"

"How the hell do I know? A guy that slimy must have left a trace somewhere."

"Check. By the way, did you ever find out what the connection was between your friend Jason Boaz and Max Finn?"

"No. I haven't had a chance. It doesn't seem too important now."

He called Faye Sylvester. The kid who answered the phone dropped it on the floor, but Faye finally picked it up.

"Hi," he said. "I was just wondering how you were."

"Busy. How about you?"

"Well, it has been hectic here. I've had a big fight

here with the DA, Marcus Dementhe,'' Tubby said proudly, "and I think I'm about to nail the sanctimonious bastard.''

"Marcus Dementhe? What's he into now?''

"You know him?''

"I'm afraid so. Did you know he was once on the board of directors of our mission?''

"No. The possibility never crossed my mind.''

"Buddy asked him to leave after they caught him sleeping with one of our girls.''

"That's terrible. How did he ever get involved in your organization?''

"That was my fault. I recommended him. You see, Marcus and I were married at the time.

"Are you there?'' she asked after thirty seconds had passed.

"Yeah,'' Tubby said. "I'm just trying to understand this picture.''

"I recognize he's a lousy human being,'' she said. "I didn't know it until the end, though. It's taken me a long time to understand this picture myself.''

"I'm trying to be delicate here. He's a despicable monster, and he's your ex-husband.''

"I know. He should be in jail.''

"He's been trying to ruin the reputations of several judges in New Orleans.''

"That wouldn't surprise me. I honestly think Marcus can deal with his own corruption only by imagining that others are more corrupt. If you stand for something good, he tries to bring you down into the mud. That's what he tried to do to me. It's taken me a lot of counseling to make me believe maybe I'm not so bad after all.''

''Was he always that way?''

''To tell you the truth, I think he was.''

''Where does that leave us?'' she asked after another long silence.

''I don't know,'' he admitted.

''Call me when you do,'' she said, and hung up.

There was a small letter tucked in the day's mail, so small that Tubby almost missed it. His name and address had been neatly handwritten in a fine script. Curious, he opened the envelope.

Dear Mr. Dubonnet,

I have decided to take my own life. The shame of what I have done and the shame I brought down upon Alvin is more than I can bear in this world.

When you read this I will be gone. You will know that I was found at the footsteps of the man who brought this grief upon me. I want him to witness this final act.

Please say good-bye for me to Alvin, and also to Cherrylynn.

Sultana Patel

Tubby took a deep breath. He started to reach for the phone, but his hand stopped in midair.

He folded the letter back into its envelope and

placed it in the top drawer of his desk, where he kept items of a personal nature.

Detective Kronke was right, he thought. You can't have a murder case without a murder.

At the Second District police station Vodka studied the paper he had just snatched from the fax machine.

"Get this," he said to Daneel. "One of the fingerprints we took off the back door of that sheet metal works came up with a match."

"Yeah? Who?"

"Marcus Dementhe, the new DA. All the elected officials get to have their prints on file."

"I guess he could have been buying some sheet metal."

Vodka just frowned at the flimsy piece of paper in his hands.

Tubby claimed his Chrysler at the city pound. Detective Kronke had cleared the way for that on condition that Tubby not call him anymore. It was a sunny day, so he picked up Raisin and they were driving around Audubon Park looking at the river.

"Lots of bodies, but no murder," Raisin commented. "Or are you going to frame him for the job?"

"Frame? Ahem. Well," Tubby replied. "At some level the guilty will pay." He watched an oil tanker round the bend while he parked the car. " 'I don't

care when they get buried if their souls go
a-blackberrying.' "

"Are you quoting Chaucer at me again?"

" 'In legal matters he was a great help, not like a
cloistered monk with a threadbare cloak, but more like
a master or a pope.' "

"You're a pope, all right," Raisin snorted.

"So how's Sapphire?" Tubby asked.

"She's doing great. She told me to pack up and get
out."

"Really?"

"Yeah. It's time to move on again."

"How do you feel about it?"

"She's right. I'm not together enough for her."

"You're writing it off?"

"Time will tell. I still like her."

"She's a very neat young woman. I learned some
things from her."

"Like what?"

"To look at people more closely than I've been
looking."

Raisin raised an eyebrow.

"I'm saying, you roam around New Orleans and you
see a lot of people you wouldn't see anywhere else. And
it definitely makes life intriguing."

A man with an Indian feather stuck in his headband
fished for bottom feeders off the sidewalk. He was eating
a sack of crawfish, and he threw a shell their way.

"Quite a revelation," Raisin said dryly.

"Well, it was for me. Sapphire kind of opened my

eyes to my surroundings. I'm feeling better about everything.''

''Fact is, Tubby, anyplace else you'd be a fish out of water. It's not the weird people that make life in New Orleans bearable. It's because those weird people tolerate you, strange as you are. You're insulated from the real world here. This is the Big Crazy, man. It's geographically incorrect. You fit right in.''

''Are you insulting me?''

Raisin just chuckled. ''Whoever said, 'In life, the race belongs to the swift,' was obviously not from New Orleans,'' he added.

''If you can't put up with termites, mosquitoes, and floods, I wouldn't urge you to live here,'' Tubby conceded.

''Personally, I think it could just be the fall weather,'' Raisin said. ''The temperature is finally dropping. Everybody feels better.''

''Everybody but you, maybe.''

''I'm working through some things,'' Raisin mumbled.

''What? Like getting older? We're all on that train together.''

''You're telling me? You've been groaning about the sand running through the hourglass for months now.''

''I'm coming to grips with all that.''

''Great. But you've accomplished some things in your life.''

''So have you.''

Raisin laughed. He lit a cigarette with a wooden match, which he then flicked toward the water.

"You know, you've got kids and everything," he said softly, exhaling smoke.

Tubby couldn't think of a snappy comeback. He watched the seagulls following a tugboat.

"But then, I should be glad just to wake up and see another sunrise."

"Me too," Tubby agreed. "It's a wonderful world. Most days."

"Louis Armstrong knew a few things, didn't he? By the way, what are you doing for Thanksgiving?"

"Don't know yet. You?"

"I'm thinking about dishing out turkey at the Ozanam Inn. Speaking of which, how long has it been since you stopped drinking?"

"Six and a half weeks."

"You look good."

"Thanks."

"Want to break your streak and go have a beer?"

"I haven't decided yet."

He started up the car, and they drove to Mike's Bar.

"There's more to life than alcohol," Tubby told him, on the way.

"Hold that thought," Raisin said.

"You know, people are a lot like stars," Tubby began.

Raisin threw his cigarette butt out the window.